Mr. Holt drew back from the cow and frowned down at his smaller companion. "I thought as how you might have picked up the scent that's been in my nostrils these past weeks."

"Scent?"

"Evil," said Mr. Holt flatly, and smote his hand lightly against the rail to emphasize his point. "That's an unfashionable word, isn't it? Well, I'm not a clever bloke—all I know's farming, but I know evil too. It's around, Sister. I can smell it on the wind...."

Also by Veronica Black:

A VOW OF SILENCE *
LAST SEEN WEARING

*Published by Ivy Books

A VOW
OF
CHASTITY

Veronica Black

IVY BOOKS • NEW YORK

Ivy Books
Published by Ballantine Books
Copyright © 1991 by Veronica Black

Library of Congress Catalog Card Number: 91-41092

ISBN 0-8041-1055-7

This edition published by arrangement with St. Martin's Press, Inc.

Manufactured in the United States of America

First Ballantine Books Edition: June 1993

ONE

✠ ✠ ✠

Sister Joan of the Order of the Daughters of Compassion sat bolt upright on her narrow bed and stared into the darkness. The dream had shocked her awake, something that rarely happened after six years in the religious life. During her novitiate there had been the occasional nightmare—usually about food, she remembered. Novices, while not kept on short commons, were fed on a diet of brown bread, vegetables, fruit and fish which was healthy but lacked the sensuality of cream cakes and the odd sherry. The food dreams had long gone and any kind of remembered dream was rare these days, which made this nightmare all the more unexpected and disturbing.

She had been standing on a railway platform, waiting—for what? for whom? In the dream she'd had no idea. She'd just been waiting as train after train roared through, not stopping, belching smoke and flame. The smoke had been so thick that it was impossible to see clearly the faces of the passengers who crowded at the windows and then the smoke had cleared and she had seen Jacob, laughing at her, beckoning her. She had gestured towards her habit and he'd laughed more immoderately, the endless train

1

rushing through his face at every window. And then she'd
glanced down and realized that she stood naked, white
skin blotched with soot, outlined with fire. And Jacob had
gone on laughing.

The darkness was disconcerting, images from her dream
still hanging in it; Jacob with the lock of black hair falling
over the high, clever brow; the long snake of iron; the
windows with the black smoke billowing up from the
wheels beneath. Usually after a gentler dream, when
she tried to hold on to it after waking, it fell back into her
mind in a tangle of grey cobweb, faint image, dying sound.
This dream—nightmare—stayed vivid, disfiguring the
dark.

It was forbidden to light the lamp save in cases of grave
necessity. Sister Joan drew up her knees under the thin
blanket and considered the matter. She wasn't in any danger of death or seriously ill and her sharp ears had caught
no sound of an intruder. On the other hand her mind was
quite gravely discomposed. If she turned over and tried
to sleep again she might slip back into the nightmare.

She decided upon a compromise, waiting until the
shapes of the few pieces of furniture in the cell materialized dimly and then rose, slipping her bare feet into the
pair of serviceable slippers at the side of the bed, reaching
for the equally practical grey dressing-gown that hung next
to her habit behind the door. Knotting the cord she was
surprised to find that her hands were trembling.

The door opened without creaking and she stood for a
moment in the corridor, grateful for the dim bulb that
burned in the light socket. Down both sides were the
closed doors of the other cells. Five on one side, four on
the other as the prioress had a larger space. Two of the
cells were empty, the convent not having its full comple-
ment of Sisters. It was a complaint echoed by other houses

in other orders. Too few suitable young women coming into the religious life. Of course quality was what mattered, Reverend Mother Dorothy said. There had been a period not too long before when the quality in this particular convent had fallen short—but that period was never mentioned. During the past year one postulant had joined the main community as a sister, not yet fully fledged as she hadn't taken her final vows, but to all intents and purposes a full member of the little group of women who lived, worked and prayed in this quiet corner of Cornwall. Sister Teresa slept noiselessly in the cell between Sister Katharine who took care of the linen and Sister Martha who did most of the gardening. A nice girl, Sister Joan thought, dragging her thoughts deliberately away from the dream. Sister Teresa helped out where she was needed during her final year of preparation. She had fine grey eyes and a pleasant manner and seemed genuinely to enjoy the religious life. Of the other three novices who had shared her time of testing Rose had decided to leave; Barbara had chosen another order in which to train; Veronica had married.

Thinking of Veronica helped to banish the nightmare. Veronica was exquisite to look at and had a nature to match. She had been sent home for a vacation and there married Johnny Russell.

"Such a loss to the religious life," Sister Hilaria had lamented gently. Privately Sister Joan had applauded the decision. Veronica and Johnny Russell made a handsome couple. They had sent a photograph of the wedding and small slabs of cake in fancy boxes. They were happy together, Sister Joan thought, and was glad for them both.

The horror of nightmare was fading. She could have turned round and quietly gone back into her cell, but her mouth was dry and her hands still shook a little. She moved out of the corridor on to the main landing that overlooked the wide front hall.

Cornwall House had been a private mansion belonging to the Tarquin family until its last owner had sold it cheaply to the Daughters of Compassion. Though it had the mingled scents of beeswax, soap and burnt-out candles that all convents seemed to acquire, Sister Joan could imagine it as it had once been, with the hall filled with well-dressed, chattering people, with curtains of scarlet and gold looped back at the long windows, with great bowls of gardenias spilling over the mirrored surfaces of the tables. She had no way of knowing if her fancies were accurate since she had been transferred here the previous year, ostensibly to help teach in the local school, in actual fact to help probe a disturbing situation that had turned out to be dynamite.

Going down the wide stairs her hand touched the satiny wood of the balustrade with a gesture that was almost sensuous. Surfaces had always fascinated her; the soft prickly surface of fur; the round whorls of blue glinting stone; the roughness of plaster—sculpture had never been her main talent but it had excited her. To convey the texture of surface in paint had been an ever constant ambition. Her talent had not matched it, a fact that had made it easier for her to choose the religious life. She had not been sacrificing a brilliant career when she entered the convent.

"Only me," Jacob had said, with his bitter, tender smile. "Only our life together."

It was the dream that had brought him back into her mind. Consciously she almost never thought of him, save now and then when Easter came round and she recalled the Passover dinner he had once cooked for her—the bitter herbs, hard boiled eggs, the shankbone of lamb, and little matzo dumplings floating in golden chicken soup.

This was nonsense and she had better get a hold on her truant thoughts. She could have taken a cup of water from the bathroom upstairs. Nice, cold water. At that moment she felt a neat slug of good whisky wouldn't have come amiss, and hastily poured it back into the bottle and substituted a mug of hot milk. It wasn't easy to crave hot milk but it was probably better for the nerves.

To her right as she stood at the foot of the stairs, double doors led into an antechamber beyond which lay the prioress' parlour; to her left another pair of doors gave on to visitors' parlour and chapel. At the foot of the main staircase a narrower door separated kitchen and infirmary from the hall. The lay Sisters slept at the back of the kitchen where two ground floor cells had been made out of pantry and buttery. At present only plump Sister Margaret who cooked for the community and did most of the shopping occupied the lay section, near where the two old nuns who occupied the infirmary, more by reason of age than sickness, spent most of their time.

Sister Joan opened the door and padded into the short corridor lit by the customary low burning bulb. The infirmary door was ajar and the sound of a gentle snoring floated out like a litany. The next door opened into a small room where the official infirmarian, Sister Perpetua, held what she was pleased to call her surgery. Here she dispensed aspirin and liniment and strong cups of tea; here were the bottles of herbal remedies with which she tried, often very successfully, to stave off the necessity to call in the local doctor. A small refrigerator held milk and various lotions that needed to be kept cool. Sister Perpetua slept upstairs in the main wing, one ear supposedly cocked for the tap on the door from Sister Margaret to inform her she was required.

There was no need to break rules by switching on the light. Sister Joan opened the refrigerator, took out the milk and poured some neatly into a beaker. It wasn't whisky and she couldn't be bothered to heat it up but it was cold and sweet and her trembling had ceased. The dream was assuming the normal place that dreams assumed, comfortably in the back of her mind.

"Oh, it's you."

Almost dropping the beaker in fright she swung about as a footstep and a soft voice sounded behind her.

"Sister Gabrielle, what are you doing out of bed?" Her voice had sharpened with alarm.

"Finding out who's out of bed," the other returned, not without humour. "Did you think I'd taken to getting up and trotting out to buy bread at three in the morning like a senile old fool?"

"No, of course not."

At eighty-four Sister Gabrielle might be the biggest gossip in the community but she was very far from senile. Now her eyes bored through the darkness as she said, "Are you a secret milkaholic, Sister Joan?"

"I had a nightmare and came down to get some milk."

"Without permission, I daresay. Well, never mind you may confess it at general confession tomorrow—later today rather. It must have been a bad nightmare."

"It was." Sister Joan drained the beaker and conscientiously rinsed it under the tap.

"Not about last year's business?"

"No, not that."

The unpleasant business that had brought her to Cornwall House in the first place had been solved, neatly tidied up and sorted away in the method of convents.

"Sometimes," said Sister Gabrielle, tapping her way to the table and sitting down on the chair there, "it helps to talk about things."

"This nightmare isn't for talking about," Sister Joan said.

"Then it probably concerns a member of the opposite sex," the old lady said. "In my young days the tribe caused me plenty of nightmares, I can tell you. It was a relief to be rid of the creatures. How old are you?"

Age was not important when one was no longer in the world. One counted the years from the time one made one's profession.

"Thirty-six," Sister Joan said meekly.

"Too young for the menopause and too old for girlish moonings," Sister Gabrielle observed. "An old lover, was he?"

"We thought about getting married," Sister Joan said, aware that in talking of her secular life she was breaking another strict rule.

"And he jilted you," Sister Gabrielle said.

"He did not!" Sister Joan's dark blue eyes flashed indignantly. "He was Jewish and he wanted his children to be Jewish which meant that I'd have to convert or there wouldn't be any marriage."

"A difficult choice." The old nun spoke with a genuine sympathy. "Judaism is a fine and strong faith. Otherwise I am sure Our Blessed Lord would have chosen to be born into some other tradition. So you parted."

"I found out that I had a different vocation," Sister Joan said. "I think that I was finding it out even before Jacob and I split up. It wasn't a case of rushing into a convent to hide a broken heart."

"It very seldom is," Sister Gabrielle said dryly, "though to hear some people talk you'd imagine convents were stuffed full of broken hearted women—those that weren't perverts, that is.''

"Sister Gabrielle!''

"Oh, how the old can shock the young when they speak their minds,'' the other mocked gently. "I was twenty-three when I entered the religious life and I didn't spend all the years before wrapped up in cottonwool. Though we weren't as frank about things in those days. So now suddenly you begin to dream about your young man.''

"I was standing on a railway platform and an endless train was rushing past with Jacob's face at every window,'' Sister Joan said. "I wasn't wearing my habit, Sister.''

"You mean you were naked. Don't be mealy-mouthed.''

"Yes.''

"In dreams trains can represent life itself moving on.'' Sister Gabrielle laced her fingers together over the knob of her walking stick. "What happened to your Jacob after you split up?''

"I don't know. He went off and married someone else, I suppose.''

"His life moved on without you. At your choice, but still—''

"I was stark naked,'' Sister Joan said, blushing at the memory.

"Without defences.'' The old woman pondered for a moment more, then said, "I think your subconscious is telling you something, something that frightens you, makes you vulnerable. Can you think of anything that's happened recently to cause it?''

"Not a thing.'' Sister Joan was frowning. "Everything is chugging along nicely at the moment. Even the children are being good—astonishingly so.''

"A sure sign that something's brewing. When you go into school on Monday have a closer look at your little angels. And pray for your old friend. Send him good thoughts."

"Thank you, Sister."

She would have liked to reach out and hold the old hand for a moment but physical contact was forbidden save on public, ceremonial occasions.

"Now I shall go back to bed," Sister Gabrielle said, rising heavily. "Between us we have broken almost every rule tonight, I imagine—include the grand silence." She went out again, her stick slowly tapping.

Sister Joan waited a moment, resisting the temptation to offer help that would be proudly rejected, and then went out herself into the hall. Sleep had fled, a rare occurrence since she generally slept like a log. A white night was best coloured in with prayer. She glided across the hall and opened the door which led into the chapel wing.

Here was the antechamber with a door leading into the nuns' half of the visitors' parlour. At the other side of the grille was space for the visitor and a side door. A corridor with windows along one side led past the parlour into the private chapel. Dim lamps burned at intervals and in the chapel itself the sanctuary lamp glowed with a steady blue flame. At the side, steps twisted up to the library and store rooms above. Sister David was combining the jobs of librarian and sacristan at the moment, scurrying from one task to the other with her rabbit nose twitching, enjoying every second of it.

Sister Joan went to her own place and knelt, fixing her eyes on the carved altar with its star-shaped monstrance, the twin candlesticks, and Communion-cup. The Tarquin family had been wealthy once, able to maintain their own chaplain. Now the chapel had come into its own again, lovingly polished by Sister David, with flowers arranged by Sister Martha whose delicate hands could not only work wonders with leaf and stem but also regularly wielded shovel and hoe and carted compost.

Balance, thought Sister Joan, is the essence of normality: yin and yang; silver and gold; night and day; man and woman. The religious life, by its very nature, was not balanced. She lived in a female atmosphere with only old Father Malone to supply a dash of masculinity when he chatted briefly with the Sisters over a cup of tea after Mass or Benediction. And Father Malone was no Rhett Butler. She bit back an irreverent grin and bowed her head, giving herself up to the silent companionship of the unseen that flowed through the quiet chapel. At least—at most there was always that to redress the balance, that sense of utter and undemanding love that transcended sexual needs.

It was past four. Though her watch was in her cell she knew the time by the faint lightening of the sky through the stained-glass windows. In an hour the rising bell would clang as Sister Margaret clumped upstairs on her flat sensible feet. There was nothing other-worldly about Sister Margaret, unlike Sister Hilaria, the novice mistress, who floated through her days on a cloud of ecstasy. There had been grave doubts expressed about allowing her to remain as novice mistress.

"A saintly soul," Sister Gabrielle had opined, "but not the type to knock all the romantic nonsense out of the heads of the postulants."

Reverend Mother Dorothy had, however, continued as before and Mother Dorothy was a sharply intelligent woman who presumably knew what she was doing. At any rate it was none of her business, she decided, and realized that the companionship had faded as her thoughts had wandered. Not abruptly or angrily but softly like a lover who is content to wait until the beloved recollects again.

A faint sound at the door made her turn her head. A plump figure, coifed and veiled, had entered and, genuflecting, seated herself in her own place, hands comfortably folded, broad face upturned as her lips moved silently.

What in the world was Sister Margaret doing in the chapel before rising bell time? Did she too, beneath her placid exterior, suffer the devils of sleeplessness? Sister Joan finished her own prayers in a somewhat distracted manner and rose, glancing towards the other, who seemed unaware of her presence.

It would be charity to wait, to find out if any human sympathy were needed. She moved to the Lady Altar and stood there uncertainly, noticing with some surprise that the vase at the feet of the Madonna statue was empty. Sister Martha was always very punctilious about keeping the vases filled even in winter, searching far afield for berried sprays and some hardy blooms, and this was spring.

Sister Margaret was getting up, genuflecting, turning towards the door, giving a slight start as she noticed the other.

"Sister, is anything wrong?" She hesitated before she spoke, mindful of the grand silence, but obviously regarding the presence of Sister Joan as sufficient excuse for the occasion to constitute an emergency.

"I thought something might be wrong for you," Sister Joan said.

"Me? Oh no, Sister, I'm fine." Sister Margaret smiled with evident relief. "No, I like to pop in here before the day starts—just for a little chat with Our Dear Lord, you know. I don't get much time for a heart to heart with all the cooking to be done—not that cooking isn't a joy. But sometimes it can get a mite lonely with no other lay sister, so a bit of a chat works wonders.''

She nodded towards the altar, her eyes serene in the plain, practical face.

Odd, Sister Joan thought, feeling suddenly much smaller, but the idea of Sister Margaret having intimate chats with the Divinity had never entered her head. Sister Margaret was the convent mainstay, managing to produce two meals a day on a limited budget, constantly on the go, her large feet clumping along the corridors.

''Do you mean He—?'' She paused, unsure how to proceed.

''Visions and stuff?'' Sister Margaret looked amused. ''Never a one. Why, I'd be scared out of my wits, I think. Not spiritual enough yet, I suppose. But we get along, He and I. Are you all right, dear?''

''Yes, thank you, Sister.''

And that's not true either. I'm so puffed up with my own concerns that I feel an insulting astonishment that a lay sister should enjoy such intimacy with the unseen that she needs no ecstasy.

''Then I'll get on.'' Sister Margaret paused, looking at the empty vase. ''Oh dear, what happened to the flowers—ever such nice daffodils they were. I remember thinking at Benediction how Our Dear Lady must be enjoying them. I'll pop out later and put some more in. Sister Martha will be upset if she sees they've gone.''

''Gone where?''

''One of the postulants likely spilled the water and disposed of the flowers,'' Sister Margaret said, looking slightly uncertain. ''While I'm about it I'd better jot down a note to buy more candles. Sometimes I think we must eat candles—they vanish so fast.''

''Do they?'' Sister Joan cast a frowning look towards

the box where the candles were kept and followed the lay sister into the corridor.

"I do beg your pardon, Sister," the other said, pausing suddenly, "but I caused you to break the grand silence by talking to you. Happily there's general confession this evening so I won't have it on my conscience for too long. Just one other thing. I'd take it very kindly if you didn't mention the little chats—I'd not want anyone to think that I was setting myself up to be singular or anything like that. So, now for the new day."

She clumped ahead, lifting the large bell from its hook by the door, beginning to ring it as she mounted the main staircase, her cheerful voice booming, "Christ is risen."

"Thanks be to God," Sister Joan responded automatically, following, closing the door of her cell behind her just as the scattered voices began to chorus their sleepy replies.

She felt sleepy herself now but two hours' prayer lay ahead before the night's fast was broken with a cup of coffee, a slice of bread and a piece of fruit, eaten standing according to the rule. She sloshed cold water over her face, dried it on the small towel, cleaned her teeth, wriggled out of nightgown and dressing-gown and into the ankle length grey habit and exchanged the cotton nightcap for coif and short veil, marvelling as she always did that she could achieve perfect neatness without the aid of a mirror. During her postulence the art of doing that as efficiently as the professed nuns had seemed as impossible an ambition as learning how to levitate.

When she re-entered the chapel she glanced at the Lady Altar and saw that the vase already held daffodils again, their golden heads drooping forlornly as if they knew that Sister Margaret's chapped and unskilful hands had pushed them in.

Saturday meant no school, no ride across the moor on Lilith's broad back. Saturday meant helping Sister David to catalogue the library which was extensive and would take several more years to get into perfect order. It meant preparing her lessons for the following week, making lists of school supplies to be obtained. It meant the general confession at the end of the day—an ordeal at the best of times but doubly to be dreaded when she had so much on her conscience.

The day went too quickly. Time always sped past when she was in the library under any circumstances and the sorting and cataloguing of the volumes bequeathed by the Tarquin family was an absorbing task.

"Anything of an equivocal nature is to be set aside for my consideration," the prioress had said.

"Out with Jackie Collins and in with Barbara Cartland," Sister Joan had murmured to Sister Teresa who had looked suitably shocked and then giggled, earning herself an icy look from Mother Dorothy.

At 12:30 was the first real meal of the day—soup in winter, salad with cheese or fish in summer, two thick slices of bread and nice cold water with a spoonful of honey since Sister Perpetua believed in its youth giving qualities.

In the afternoon she took herself back to the library armed with a pile of exercise books and a red pencil. The little local school where she taught had been endowed originally for the Tarquin family's tenants whose children found it difficult in the era before buses to get to the school in Bodmin. It still remained, attended by the younger children of local farmers and intermittently by the Romany children when they weren't off playing truant and poaching. Sister Joan enjoyed the work though she often wondered if anything she tried to drum into the heads of her pupils would ever be of the slightest use to them in after years.

For homework during the week she had set them a short composition on their favourite flowers. The task had been completed and handed in by six out of her ten pupils, which wasn't too bad when she remembered the groan the boys had sent skywards. Two of the entries could scarcely be classified as homework, however. One was smudged with so much ink that it was impossible to read; the other contained a statement of rebellion.

> *I cant make up stuff about flewers becaus I am NOT QUEER,*
> *Yurs respectful,*
> *Conrad Smith.*

Conrad was thirteen and should have been sent regularly to school years before. He came from the less law-abiding branch of the large Romany family camped out on the moor, and only sat in her classroom now because of the threats of his mother who was sick of being chased by the school inspector. Conrad, thought Sister Joan, showed a pleasing spirit of independence, and turned with less enjoyment to Madelyn Penglow's book in which she had carefully copied the over familiar lines by Wordsworth, apparently under the serene misapprehension that her teacher would regard them as her own invention.

Two of the others had drawn pictures of rather stylized-looking birds—or perhaps they were meant to be flowers? The remaining piece of work was also about daffodils, which at this season was hardly surprising. What was surprising was its content.

They say daffodils are trumpets.
I say daffodils are strumpets,
And lads are bad and girls black pearl,
And little roses full of worms

Neatly written, properly spelt, and not from any poetry collection that Sister Joan had ever seen. Samantha Olive's book. She was new to the district, her parents having just moved here. A slim child of eleven or twelve with bright green eyes in an otherwise ordinary little face. Sister Joan hadn't paid much heed to her, deeming it better to let the child settle in before she started assessing her. The doggerel rhyme was not what she would have expected.

She put the books aside, drew the copy of the timetable towards her and began to jot down ideas for the coming week—a nature ramble, a spelling bee, a talk about Philip Sidney to get across the idea that not all poets were effeminate—the bell for private study rang. Time to get out the journal that every Sister kept and note down her sins, her meditation thoughts, her private heart—all useful evidence in the unlikely event of the cause for canonisation being introduced for any of them in the future.

I accuse myself, Sister Joan wrote neatly in the thick, black-covered notebook, *of having dreamed erotically—* was a dream a sin? Had it ever been erotic? More frightening and embarrassing, she considered. Not erotically then. She inked out the work, apple-pied the offending letters as the prioress was sometimes constrained to do, writing the words "apple pie" over parts of letters and books that might prove disturbing or unsuitable for more susceptible nuns to read.

I accuse myself of not taking sufficient time to consider my sins and thus of being forced to cross out words, wasting space and defacing the book. I accuse myself of dwell-

ing overmuch on a nightmare concerned with things quite irrelevant to my present situation—

"I never thought I'd end up as an irrelevancy," Jacob said inside her head, his eyes tenderly mocking.

She rubbed him out of her head and wrote on.

I accuse myself of having left my sleeping quarters, gone down to the kitchen, and drunk a mug of milk without permission and of having broken the grand silence and of having incited two of my Sisters in Christ to have followed my example—not strictly true since Sister Gabrielle had broken silence first, but she was old and might be excused on the grounds of forgetfulness.

I accuse myself of spiritual pride and aridity, and pray God and you, my dear Sisters, to forgive and understand these my faults.

If, at some future date, the devil's advocate came looking for reasons why Sister Joan wasn't suitable to be raised to the altars he'd find lots of evidence here, she thought.

The bell rang again. She picked up the journal and descended the stairs, sliding into her place as the rest of the community filed in, all except prioress and novice mistress clutching their books. The two senior members of the convent were excluded from general confession lest anything they felt constrained to say denigrate their standing in the eyes of the others. A prioress was elected for five years after which she returned into the body of the community and took her place at general confession with the rest. Sister Joan wondered if it was worth wasting any hopes on the unlikely chance of her ever being elected prioress or put in charge of any novices and decided not to waste her time.

Mother Dorothy, hunched and plain, rimless spectacles perched on a nose that was nearly as sharp as her tongue, came in. Sister Joan, kneeling with the rest, wondered gloomily what penance this little lot was going to earn her. About two hundred Hail Mary's and salt in her coffee for a month probably. Mother Dorothy belonged to the old school of discipline and hadn't yet decided if she was going to accept Vatican Two.

I accuse myself of levity and uncharitable thoughts about my dear Sister, Sister Joan thought, rising, beginning the Confiteor. She would save those two for the following week. A thin shaft of sunlight broke free from the prism of stained glass and dyed the daffodils in the vase on the Lady Altar a sinister red.

Daffodils are strumpets, Sister Joan's mind whispered the phrase as her lips shaped Latin.

TWO

✠ ✠ ✠

Monday morning had come as a relief. Usually Sister Joan cherished the slow, quiet hours of the Sabbath. On Sunday only the bare minimum of secular work was done; in addition to the two extra hours of prayer there were two hours of recreation instead of one, and stretches of spare time when it was possible to read and write letters.

Sister Joan, however, had been constrained, after general confession, to spend the whole day in chapel.

"With your faults so heavy on your conscience you will not wish to partake of the pleasures of the Sabbath," Mother Dorothy had said. "Your meals you may take in the kitchen. I am sure you will want to spend the day fasting, however."

Sister Joan was equally sure that she wouldn't want to spend the day fasting, but she controlled the rebellious flash of her dark blue eyes and bowed submissively.

"What a treat," Sister Margaret whispered in passing, "to spend the whole day in chapel with no distractions."

Her own breaking of the grand silence had been met with shocked gasps from the two postulants and an icy lecture from Mother Dorothy. Sister Gabrielle had been told to set her own penance. That she would apply a harsh one to herself went without saying.

The day had crawled on leaden feet, through the morning meditation, the mass, the long hours of solitude. Today the companionship of the Unseen was entirely fled; Sister Joan knelt alone, combatting cramp by making the Stations of the Cross at regular intervals, unhappily aware that true contrition still lay a long way off. Towards late afternoon her stomach had started growling discontentedly.

No, it was a relief to wake up on Monday and start the week afresh. On Wednesday Father Malone came to hear confession and she would have to tell her sins all over again. Father's penances, however, were light compared with those inflicted by Mother Dorothy.

She had just mounted the placid Lilith for the ride to the schoolhouse when Mother Dorothy had appeared unexpectedly at the stable gate, her pinched face emphasized by the sunlight.

"Good morning, Sister Joan." Her dry voice had held neither praise nor blame.

"Reverend Mother Dorothy." Sister Joan hastily pulled down the skirt of her habit, apt to ride up when she was in the saddle.

"I believe that it would be quite consistent with the rule if you were to wear a pair of—long trousers beneath your skirt when you ride to and from school," Mother Dorothy said. "More comfortable and less likely to give rise to scandal. I shall tell Sister Margaret to purchase two pairs in your size."

"Thank you, Reverend Mother." Sister Joan had smiled her gratitude.

"I used to ride myself when I was a girl," Mother

Dorothy said. "A most enjoyable exercise but only when suitably clad. Good morning, Sister."

"Good morning, Reverend Mother."

Sister Joan had watched the small, hunched figure turn and walk back towards the kitchen quarters. Generosity of spirit manifested itself in strange guises.

Now, mistress of her own domain, she sat at the large desk in the single classroom that comprised the local school and let her eyes rove over her pupils. There were only ten who came now to the school on the moor, and at eleven or twelve years old they would move on into the State school at Bodmin, catching the bus every morning, returning at teatime. At least the farmers' children would do that; the Romanies, she suspected, would find excuses to stay away.

The farming children—represented by three boys and two girls sat in one block, in an instinctive drawing away from the gypsies that Sister Joan deplored but hadn't yet succeeded in combatting. Madelyn and David Penglow sat together, faces scrubbed clean, fair hair and blue eyes making them look like twins drawn in a child's storybook. The polite manners and pleasant smiles couldn't really compensate for the fact that the Penglows were dreadful little prigs, Sister Joan thought. She had a softer spot for Billy Wesley who was as mischievous as a cartload of monkeys but had twice the Penglows' intelligence. Next to him Timothy Holt was already fidgeting, his eyes wandering to the clock on the wall. Tim considered any lessons that didn't have a direct connection with agriculture to be a waste of time. The odd one out in the "farming" group, as Sister Joan thought of them, was the newcomer, Samantha Olive. She had been scarcely a month in the school and still sat slightly apart, shifting her desk slightly before she sat down in the morning as if to emphasize her

isolation. A plain child, though not so plain that her face
became interesting, only the cat-green eyes alive as they
watched from a curtain of thick, pale lashes. Sister Joan
realized there was something unnerving about that
unwavering, eleven-year-old scrutiny.

The Romanies sat across the aisle, though "sat" was a
relative word, since they preferred to slide down on to the
floor or squirm their legs around their chairs as if they
were poised for instant flight. For a wonder the five of
them were present, even thirteen-year-old Conrad sitting
upright with shining morning face. His sister, Hagar, jet
pigtails touching the desk before her, sat next to him.
Hagar ought to start going to the Bodmin school, Sister
Joan thought. She was twelve and looked older, her breasts
already well developed, a certain knowing look in her eyes
that deepened when they were turned on any of the boys.
Hagar, however, was devoted to her brother and certainly
wouldn't attend regularly at any establishment where he
refused to go.

The Lees, cousins and rivals of the Smiths, completed
her small quota of pupils. Petroc sprawled at his desk,
already yawning—the result, probably, of a night's illicit
rabbit snaring; Edith and Tabitha huddled side by side,
looking like two of the rabbits that Petroc regularly hunted.
At six and seven they were still greatly in awe of anything
to do with education—a happy state of affairs that Sister
Joan knew from experience wouldn't last long.

She drew the homework books towards her and gave
what she hoped was an encouraging smile.

"I asked you to write about your favourite flowers,"
she began, "and the work that was handed in pleased me
on the whole. Petroc, you'll have to copy yours out again,
I'm afraid, because you got the inkwell muddled up with
the paper. Conrad, it was thoughtful of you to explain why

you didn't hand in any work, but the explanation won't do. This week I shall be telling you about Sir Philip Sidney who was a very brave soldier and a poet—also married. Madelyn, your work was very neat but you copied the poem from a book, didn't you?''

"No, Sister." The blue eyes were limpid. "David copied it and then he read it to me."

"You both copied the same poem? Then where is David's work?"

"We didn't want to hand in two the same, Sister, in case you got bored," David said pedantically, "so I tore the pages out of my book."

"Logical, I suppose," Sister Joan said, "but in future I'd like you both to work by yourselves and try to compose something of your own."

The twins, unable to contemplate a separate mental existence, stared back at her blankly.

"Timothy, your drawing was very good though it wasn't quite what I'd asked for." Sister Joan nodded at the child pleasantly. He had drawn what he saw, neatly and unimaginably dully, but she had a soft place in her heart for those who expressed themselves in paint rather than words. Tabitha had also sent in a drawing—less neat and accurate but infinitely more colourful. Edith hadn't sent anything in. She told her gently that she must try to do the homework, aware that any harsher scolding would bring the tears flooding to the little girl's sloe-black eyes, and spoke rather more sharply to Hagar about her failure to do the set task, knowing that her words were making no impression upon the girl at all. Hagar merely smiled, one side of her full mouth curving in mute contempt, as Conrad said quickly and loyally, "Hagar don't mean to be lazy, Sister. She has lots to do at 'ome—washing and cooking and the like, and she needs time to enjoy."

To enjoy what? Sister Joan thought, her eye measuring the jut of budding breasts. There was something in Hagar's scornful little smile that hinted at pity for herself. She wanted to shake the child, to inform her roundly that the religious life didn't unsex anyone, but Hagar wouldn't have understood.

"Try to enjoy doing a little homework occasionally," she advised. "Billy, one of these days you are going to astonish us all by actually doing some homework. Could you make it soon?"

"Can we write about something else next time?" Billy asked promptly.

"This coming week you can all write—write not draw—a few sentences about the person you admire most—admire means wanting to be like them, Edith. Just a few words, of your own and not copied."

"Alive or dead?" Billy inquired with as much interest as if he were actually going to do the homework.

"Whichever you like," Sister Joan said. "Samantha, did you read the poem you sent somewhere in a book?"

"No, Sister." The voice was neat and precise.

"It was—unusual," Sister Joan said cautiously. "Nicely written and spelled, if a bit—morbid. Perhaps you should try to write happier pieces?"

"Yes, Sister." The green eyes held her own blue ones for a moment and then were lowered.

"So!" Mentally resolving to look more closely into the child's home background Sister Joan spoke brightly, telling herself that cheerfulness was contagious. And that, she realized abruptly, was the trouble. Her pupils who generally exasperated her for half of the time were simply too quiet, too solemn, too attentive. She held the realization at the back of her mind while she outlined the week's projects. One of her most difficult tasks lay in welding together a group of children between the ages of six and thirteen into a class following roughly the same curriculum. Nature walks, talks about events that the older ones would have read in the newspapers, opportunities for them to express themselves in drawing or singing, all these took precedence over formal lessons though she took care to include some of those too. Sister David who had helped out as her assistant was now full time convent librarian and there were times when Sister Joan missed her help exceedingly.

She thrust aside the selfish desire for less work and talked on enthusiastically about the project she had dreamed up just before going to bed.

"A history of the district with a coloured map and drawings of the animals and the plants that are found here and pictures of the houses, and then bits about the people who lived here long ago. We can make a series of folders or even an exhibition for your parents to come and see."

"For fifty pence," David suggested.

"Well, I'm not sure about that—we'll see. Now we'd better do some arithmetic," she said firmly, and prepared to wrestle with the multiplication tables. Apparently nobody learned them these days but it was the only way she knew of fixing numbers in youthful heads.

When break came she dismissed the children, a slight frown creasing her brow as she saw how obediently they rose, girls filing out ahead of boys. It was what she was always trying to instil into them but the lack of the usual scramble to the door was unnerving.

"Conrad, one moment, please." Her voice and beckoning finger detained her eldest pupil.

"Yes, Sister?" The boy turned back, looking at her expectantly. Tall and broad for his age, she judged, with little of the wiry slenderness of the other Romany children. There were rumours that his mother had been less than particular about her partners and that Conrad's father was not the thin, stooped Jeb Smith who had deserted his family some months before but a travelling man, a tinker with whom she'd briefly taken up in the years when she had still been pretty.

"Everybody seems very good these days," she hazarded. "I was wondering why?"

"Ain't we supposed to be good then?" Conrad demanded.

"Yes, of course. Of course you are. It merely occurred to me that you were all being very good," she said, keeping the look of enquiry on her face.

"Reckon we just caught it," Conrad said after a moment's thought.

"Well, if it's only goodness that you catch then we ought to be grateful, I suppose."

"Yes, Sister." He gazed at her steadily from under his cowlick of dark hair.

"Yes, well—thank you, Conrad."

The dismissal, she knew, sounded feeble but she couldn't think of anything else to say. Perhaps the unnaturally good behaviour, which she realized had been going on for some time, was merely a sign that they were growing up, becoming more responsible. She collected up the arithmetic exercises, wiped the blackboard and went out of the room, past the small cloakroom to the outside where neither wall nor quadrangle separated the building from the moor.

The school had originally been endowed by the Tarquin family for the children of the tenants. It was still administered by a Trust that provided books and paid for the repair and upkeep of the building. But the number of pupils was steadily diminishing; in another year or two there would no longer be any reason to keep it open. She tried to explore her own feelings, to decide whether or not she would regret it. She wasn't a trained teacher, but the work was interesting and she'd established a rapport with some of the children. Too close a rapport, perhaps? There was always the danger of losing the detachment that was part of the religious life. These children were not her own children and the teaching was only secondary to her life, the modest salary paid out of the Trust going directly to the convent.

The children were split as usual into two groups, Romanies and farmers' offspring. Usually they scampered about, young voices echoing over the moor, but this morning the two small groups clustered together, talking quietly, eating the bags of crisps and sweets provided from home. One or two of the little ones had already started on their lunchtime sandwiches. There were no facilities for the provision of a midday meal apart from a kettle where one could boil water for a hot drink or a packet soup.

Not all the children were joined into the groups. The new child, Samantha Olive, had wandered off a little way to where a solitary beech spread protecting branches over the mossy turf. She stood with her back to the others, staring out across the waves and dips of the moor.

Sister Joan strolled towards her, attitude casual.

"It is a lovely view, isn't it?" she said, reaching the child's side. "When I am troubled I like to stand and look out over the grass and the heather to where the land meets the sky. It makes my own worries seem very small."

"Does it, Sister?" A polite, indifferent little voice, the profile unyielding.

Sister Joan sighed, saying, "You are still settling in here, I daresay. In a few weeks it will feel as if you've always lived here. Let me see. Your parents took over Farren Farm, didn't they?''

"Yes, Sister.''

"Do your parents like the district? It must seem very quiet after the city.'' The Olives weren't farmers but had come originally from up north somewhere. The child still had the flat vowel sounds of Lancashire in her voice, though they were scarcely perceptible. She came from what might be termed an upper-class background, Sister Joan thought, remembering the slim, stylish woman who had brought Samantha to school.

"My husband has a fancy to write a book or something of that nature.'' Mrs. Olive had possessed a languid, die-away voice. Her eyes, green between mascara'd lashes, had held a tolerant amusement at the idea of her husband writing a book. Or that was how Sister Joan had interpreted it at the time, feeling a sudden sympathy for the absent Mr. Olive. Now she wondered if Mrs. Olive hadn't been laughing at her, a woman the same age as herself but so differently clad in an ankle-length grey habit with short white veil and white wimple, her legs encased in black tights and sensible laced shoes, the narrow gold band on her left hand a symbol of her spiritual marriage. In contrast Mrs. Olive wore a suit that was probably a Chanel with a green scarf that echoed her eyes, her long ash blond hair coiled and folded like wings at the back of her sleek head. Only her skin detracted from her looks, pitted with the tiny marks of severe teenage acne. Sister Joan had instinctively put up her hand to her own smooth, glowing complexion and then felt ashamed. Personal vanity had no place in the life of a Sister of the Order of the Daughters of Compassion.

"It would be possible for me to take Samantha to the school in Bodmin but I like the idea of a little rural school," Mrs. Olive had continued. "It will ease her more gradually into country life."

"She is eleven, isn't she?" Sister Joan had frowned slightly. "You know, she has to go to the State School when she's twelve at the latest. We simply don't have the staff or the facilities here to provide a complete senior education."

"A couple of terms will suffice." Mrs. Olive had sounded more bored than ever. "Our au pair will be dropping her off every morning and picking her up in the afternoon."

Now, glancing at the child's remote little profile, Sister Joan said, "Is everything all right at home, Samantha? Your parents are well?"

"Yes, thank you, Sister."

"And you like it here? With the other children?" Getting information was like wading through deep mud with heavy boots on.

"I like it very much, Sister."

For the first time there was a lilt in the cool, dry voice, a quick flash of a smile.

"You don't have any brothers and sisters, do you?" Sister Joan said.

Samantha shook her head briefly.

"Then it must be pleasant for you to have companions," Sister Joan said, wondering where to go from there. Was there, indeed, anywhere to go? There was no accounting for the direction a young imagination might take. She recalled that as a schoolgirl herself she had spent one whole summer copying the epitaphs from gravestones and lulling herself to sleep with pleasant fantasies of herself, suitably pale and beautiful, dying of a broken heart or sliding into a decline like Beth in *Little Women*.

"Oh yes, Sister," said Samantha.

"Then perhaps we ought to start a game or something," Sister Joan said, conceding victory to her—ridiculous to think of an eleven-year-old kid as an opponent. She reached out, took a small, limp, unresponsive hand and started back towards the others, saying in the loudly hearty tones of a particular games mistress she recalled from her own schooldays.

"We'll be indoors again soon enough, so let's play rounders for a while. Conrad, go into the cupboard and bring out the stumps. Billy, you help him. We can mark out the ground with a bit of chalk."

To her relief something like childish enthusiasm returned to the children. For the next half hour they ran, hit out at the ball, argued scores like normal youngsters. Which, she reminded herself firmly, was exactly what they were. This unusual meekness was a phase and instead of worrying about it she ought to be thanking her stars that she had managed to instil the rudiments of good conduct into so diverse a group.

"You were out that time, Samantha." She pulled her thoughts back to the present, waving towards the girl.

"She was in," David said. "She was in, Sister."

"No, dear. She was definitely run out," Sister Joan said.

"Was I?" Samantha asked not her own side but the opposing side. There was the earnest desire to know on her small, plain face.

The Romanies shifted their feet, hesitating. Then Hagar called, "In. Samantha was in."

"Out," said Sister Joan and was instantly engulfed in protest from both sides.

"All right, all right. In, if you insist," she said at last in exasperation, "but if this is a ploy to spin out break time it won't work because I'd already decided to make this a games period anyway.''

And don't forget to make a note of that for your next general confession, she advised herself silently.

Samantha's team won which was hardly surprising since Samantha herself was never run out even by the long legged Petroc, and her wildest swipes at the ball were all acclaimed as hits. Perhaps it was the children's way of making a newcomer feel welcome, but Samantha had already been at the school for several weeks, and in any case Sister Joan had never before noticed any signs of excessive kindness to new pupils in any of the others. For the moment the riddle would have to remain.

The dinner-hour and the rest of the afternoon passed. The children ate their sandwiches and drank the cups of tea that she brewed up on the table at the back of the classroom—it ought to have been milk, she supposed, and made a mental note to order more. She talked about Sir Philip Sidney with the uneasy feeling that despite her efforts most of the boys still regarded him as a bit of a sissy; set the older ones to labelling some blank maps while she gathered the little ones around for a simple spelling bee; reminded them about the project she'd mentioned earlier, and saw the hands of the clock stand at 3:30 with more relief than she'd have thought possible at the beginning of the day.

"Time for the afternoon prayer, children." Her tone was joyful.

"A simple morning and afternoon prayer, Sister Joan," Mother Dorothy had instructed. "Not all the children are Catholics. Nothing unconventional or novel."

The children rose, virtue shining on their faces. Too much virtue for small souls to bear. She composed her own face, bowed her head, recited the short prayer and crossed herself, some of the children following suit. Samantha, she noticed, was not among them. There was no surprise in that since the Olives weren't Catholic. All the Romany children crossed themselves though she suspected that they all forgot their Catholicism the moment they were out of the school door.

Hooting from the track announced the arrival of the pick-up truck in which some of her pupils rode home. Further off a sleek car had drawn up. Samantha headed towards it, not running and tumbling but walking sedately. A nicely brought up child, Sister Joan reflected, and turned to greet the wiry dark man who jumped down from the truck.

"Good afternoon, Mr. Lee. I haven't seen you in quite a while." She shook the hard, dark hand.

"Been inside, ain't I?" the man said. "Three months of picking up something that the magistrates wouldn't have paid ten pence for on a good day. Injustice."

"It fell off the back of a lorry, I suppose?"

"Aye, something of that nature." He grinned, one rebel acknowledging another. "You know, Sister, I've told you before if you ever need anything cheap—cigarettes now—"

"I don't smoke."

"And quite right too, Sister. Nasty, unhealthy habit," he agreed. "But if you ever were to fancy a nip of whisky, say? Just tip me the wink."

"If I ever do I will," she promised, "but it's doubtful. It's very doubtful, Mr. Lee."

"Well, if you do, let me know. Come on, kids. Home's the word. Hope they've been good, Sister."

"Perfectly good," Sister Joan said.

"Then there's mischief brewing," said Mr. Lee. "Depend on it, Sister."

He saluted her and turned to chivvy the Romanies into the truck. Further off Samantha had reached the car and ducked into the back seat. The au pair brought her and picked her up every day. Sister Joan had glimpsed blonde hair and a very short skirt and allowed herself to wonder briefly if Mr. or Mrs. Olive had engaged her. Not that it was any of her business.

The other children went out, running and shouting. At least their docility didn't carry on after school hours, she thought. Didn't carry on once Samantha Olive was out of the way. Silly to think there could possibly be a connection.

Tidying the classroom, wiping the board, took only a few minutes. She locked up, went to the lean-to shed to get Lilith who greeted her with a whinny of pleasure. She would ask for permission to visit the children's parents, she decided. To call upon the Olives alone would be to pick out Samantha, focus attention on her. There was no need to lie to Mother Dorothy. The project she had envisaged might well lead to a small exhibition, a Parents' Day, something of that nature, and the parents themselves might well be involved.

Mounting up, thinking of the trousers that had been promised with renewed gratitude, she rode back to the convent. Around her the moors were quick and green, with the wild harebells that carpeted them already dancing in the breeze and the berries of the rowan tiny rubies against the darker green.

The convent had been a stately home for the local squires. She never tired of that first gracious view of the mullioned windows sparkling in the grey, ivy clad stone, the high enclosure wall where honeysuckle hung its yellow-cream fingers with their tips of scarlet. Her Mother House, where she had done her postulancy, her novitiate, been received for first temporary and then final vows, had stood in a narrow street. From the garden at the back she had seen only the sky with no open vistas. With luck she would spend the rest of her life here, be laid finally to rest in the convent cemetery where other nuns slept their deep and dreamless slumbers.

Dismounting at the main gates, always held hospitably open, she looped Lilith's rein over her arm and walked up the drive, trying to attain the happy medium between unseemly haste and idle loitering. After her recent shocking transgressions it behoved her to move carefully. Her mouth quirked into an irrepressible grin as she recalled the shock on the other faces as she made her confession. Her faults had certainly put everybody else's in the shade—which was certainly no cause for self congratulation.

"Did you have a good day, Sister Joan?"

The prioress again. Mother Dorothy, despite her age, was not the sort of woman who sat in her own quarters, and letting the even tenor of convent routine flow around her was clearly inimical to her nature. She preferred to bustle round with it—unless she had decided to keep a close eye on Sister Joan for fear she take it into her head to do something really scandalous.

"A very good day, thank you, Mother Dorothy."

"Don't forget to get yourself measured for the riding trousers." The sharp face peered up at her from between the rounded shoulders.

"No, Mother. Thank you, Mother."

"They are for modesty's sake," Mother Dorothy said severely, "not a personal indulgence."

"Of course not, Mother."

"Lilith enjoys her outings, I think." The other stroked the velvety nose. "Of course her name is most unfortunate—but then as she was named a long time ago I daresay she would not respond to anything new.''

''She doesn't always respond to her own name,'' Sister Joan said, with a grin. ''This old mare can be obstinate when she's a mind.''

''Then you must suit each other very well,'' Mother Dorothy said, the dryness of her tone indicating a joke.

''Mother, would it be possible for me to visit the parents of my pupils?'' Sister Joan took advantage of the momentary relaxation.

''For what reason?''

Sister Joan explained carefully about the project she had in mind.

''Rather ambitious, don't you think?'' The prioress frowned. ''Will it advance their education?''

''I believe so, Mother. To learn something about local history will make them use their eyes and ears more alertly, and of course as there will be some extra work involved— some of the children will require some help from their parents. And if there is to be a Parents' Day, naturally I would appreciate the co-operation of the adults.''

''If it doesn't interfere with your religious life, Sister, then I have no objection,'' her Superior said. ''In fact the idea appeals to me. So few children come to the school now and the value of the original Trust Fund has not kept pace with modern inflation, that within the year I may close the school altogether.''

''Yes, Mother Dorothy.''

Though it was news she had expected she was unable to summon a smile.

''We shall find some other useful occupation for you, Sister,'' the prioress said.

''Thank you, Mother.'' Sister Joan led Lilith into the stable.

Feeding the mare, rubbing her down, washing her own hands took up the next half hour. It was past 4:30. At this hour the Sisters were generally in their cells, examining their consciences. Sister Joan turned instead in the direction of the chapel. She hadn't lied to Mother Dorothy about the reason she wished to visit the parents but she had certainly withheld a part of the truth, if it was truth and not merely her own overstrained imagination. Remembering her dream of the previous night she feared that some very odd things were going on in her subconscious.

The chapel was quiet and sunlit. Slipping into her pew, kneeling with bowed head, she felt her own restless thoughts slow and mellow. Perhaps she had allowed her keen interest in the school to override her detachment. The dismay with which she had heard the pronouncement that it might close sooner than she had expected had been out of proportion to the effect it ought to have had on her. When the school closed the pupils would move on and quickly forget her, and she would be given work commensurate with her talents and the needs of the Order.

But please not sorting the laundry, her lips moved silently.

She raised her head to the sunlit altar and stared at the empty space on it. Not spiritually empty as it had seemed during her penance but physically denuded of the heavy silver crucifix that stood between the twin candlesticks. Behind it was the locked cupboard where the Host was kept. At mass Father Malone moved the crucifix to one side in order to unlock the door. Sister David cleaned and polished everything in the chapel twice a week—on Tuesdays and Saturdays. Today was Monday and there was no reason for anything to be missing.

She rose from her knees and went rapidly across to the

unlocked side door which gave access to the visitors' side of the parlour and thence into the side yard through which one gained the bridle path beyond the wall. The doors were kept open from early morning until the grand silence. Though the Order was semi-cloistered any member of the public who felt the need to pray in the chapel was free to do so. Very few availed themselves of the privilege since the parish church was more conveniently reached.

She would have to tell someone what had happened before someone else came in and discovered the loss. The thought that Sister Hilaria might have borrowed the crucifix while in one of her ecstasies occurred to her and was as swiftly dismissed. Sister Hilaria was delicately made, incapable of lifting anything heavy without help.

She hurried back into the main hall in time to see the door of Mother Dorothy's room close firmly. The merest whisper of voices reaching her through the oak panels reminded her that at this hour the prioress instructed the postulants who were escorted from the separate building they occupied beyond the disused tennis court for an hour's spiritual consent. Nothing short of fire or sudden death was allowed to interfere with that. She stood irresolutely for a few moments, then turned back. The crucifix was missing and nothing was likely to make any difference to the situation if she waited an hour. An hour's wait would also be good discipline for her. Sister Joan, who knew only too well that she was apt to rush in where no self-respecting angel would venture, drew a long breath and walked slowly the length of the chapel corridor into the chapel again, genuflecting to the altar, raising her head to see the sunlight beaming down on the large crucifix which shone as brightly as if it had never been missing at all.

THREE

✠ ✠ ✠

"If you occasionally stopped to think," she had been told more than once by her novice mistress in the days before her final profession, "you would find life easier, Sister."

So think! Daffodils taken from the Lady Altar and not returned, too many candles being used, a heavy crucifix taken and put back. For what possible reason? Go on thinking! Schoolchildren who suddenly begin to behave like angels, a verse written by an eleven year old that has about it a miasma of—don't let that imagination of yours run away with you, Sister Joan.

"You cannot possibly expect to get round all the parents in one evening," Mother Dorothy said. "It would be far too tiring for Sister Margaret."

"Sister Margaret?" Sister Joan looked surprised.

"Sister Margaret will naturally accompany you." The prioress looked surprised in her turn. "My dear child, you didn't fancy that you were going to gallop alone round the neighbourhood like some latter-day Paul Revere, did you?"

Sister Joan, who had fancied something of the sort, blushed.

"Sister Margaret will drive you wherever you wish to go, but I would advise splitting the visits into two evenings or you will never be back by eight o'clock."

"Nuns," Jacob had once said, "go everywhere in pairs, like cruets."

"I wouldn't want to inconvenience Sister Margaret," she said.

"Sister Margaret will be very pleased," Mother Dorothy said firmly. "She loves driving the car and a round of visits will be a real treat for her. Just check with her as to when it will suit her best. I would advise as soon as possible. When one has envisaged a somewhat ambitious project it is always sensible to get the basic details fixed firmly as quickly as is practical."

Resigned to being one half of a cruet Sister Joan duly consulted Sister Margaret whose round face beamed with pleasure.

"What a treat! The little bits and pieces you tell us about the children are so interesting that it will be a real delight to meet the parents. And driving at night is such an adventure, isn't it? When I took my test the instructor said that everybody ought to get some experience of twilight driving, so this is a marvellous opportunity."

"You'd have done better to suggest that I drive you," Sister Perpetua said. "That way you'd be sure of getting there and back in one piece. However, I shall have a tot of brandy for shock ready in the infirmary when you get back."

Her freckled white face flushed with laughter as she presented her witticism. Sister Joan, refrained from reminding everybody that she was a perfectly competent driver, also refrained from warning any of her pupils about the intending visit. She had a fancy to see the parents of

Samantha Olive before they had composed their faces into
the expression with which most lay people greeted nuns.

"Where are we to go first, Sister Joan? I am entirely at
your disposal." Sister Margaret beamed at her as they sat
in the shabby old jalopy that did duty as convent car.

Sister Joan glanced at the list she had made.

"I thought we might go to the Lees and the Smiths
first," she said.

"Oh, that will be very pleasant. Such a nice drive over
the moors in the late afternoon."

Sister Margaret bent eagerly to the ignition and an instant later the car shot backwards.

"Wrong gear," Sister Margaret said. "So fortunate
there wasn't anybody standing behind us. Our Dear Lord
is so good in little matters like that."

Sister Joan hoped fervently that He would continue to
be good as Sister Margaret drove with gay abandon down
the drive and turned on to the track. How she had passed
her test was a miracle in itself.

The Romanies camped, when they were not on their
annual travelling, on a high, flat stretch of ground past
which an unexpected river meandered lazily to lose itself
in a deep quiet pool fringed with willow. The camp itself
was rather less romantic, being a *mélange* of cooking
smells and barking dogs and piles of old tin cans, spring
mattresses, kettles, iron rails and similar junk, all due to
be sorted, loaded and sold to scrap merchants.

"Why, how nice! Here is Padraic," Sister Margaret
said, drawing up with a fine flourish that sent half a dozen
chickens squawking wildly in several directions.

"Who?" Sister Joan asked, puzzled.

Her query was answered, not in words, but by the arrival of Mr. Lee who loped over to open the door and

assist Sister Margaret out with as much ceremony as if she were a visiting duchess.

"Well now, ain't this a treat! Two holy ladies at once and just in time for a mug of tea. Children not been getting up to anything, I hope?"

"No, on the contrary," Sister Joan said quickly. "They've been very good recently. I came to discuss a school project I have in mind to do for which I may need some help from the parents."

"Any help I can give." But he looked slightly uneasy. "Not that I was ever very much at the education. I says to my two girls—'Get education and then the world's your own.' Doing all right then, are they?"

"Tabitha is starting to read very prettily," Sister Joan assured him, "and Edith has a lovely singing voice. Of course they're both still very young but I have high hopes of them. Even though they're little I'm sure that they can contribute to the project. I thought perhaps they could make some little raffia baskets, dried flower posies, traditional Romany crafts. The project is to be a history of the district, you see."

"We buy plastic bags in the supermarket," Padraic said, looking alarmed. "More modern, you see."

"Perhaps their mother—?" Sister Joan began.

"Well now, the wife isn't too grand these days." He looked more uncomfortable. "Not up to doing the chores or taking the interest she should. But if you want dead flowers and raffia baskets then those you shall have. Ain't nothing too good for them dear Sisters."

"As I well know," Sister Margaret said. "I have so much cause to be grateful to you, Padraic."

"What's a bit of fish between friends, eh, Sister Margaret?" He dug her in the ribs with his elbow, a gesture that would have been intensely painful had not her ribs been so well cushioned.

"We all enjoyed it very much," she assured him. "I served it with a nice caper sauce."

"Would that," Sister Joan enquired, "have been the salmon we had last week? On the occasion that Mother Dorothy said she didn't know how you contrived to stretch the housekeeping allowance so far?"

"Oh, that was Mother Dorothy's little jest, Sister," her companion said. "She knows very well that Padraic sometimes brings a little present over—so kind of him."

"Very." Sister Joan wondered whether it would be tactless to enquire as to whether Padraic Lee had a salmon fishing licence and decided that it would be.

They had reached a large caravan, its door closed. As Padraic hesitated Sister Margaret said, "There really isn't any need to disturb Mrs. Lee. There is nothing nicer than a drink of tea in the open air."

"Coming right up, Sisters. Also two good solid chairs, none of your canvas rubbish. The girls are playing somewhere. Petroc! Go and get Tabby and Edie and then come along yourself. I'm about to brew up so it'll be good and hot."

Also strong, Sister Joan thought, choking slightly over the mug. There must have been several spoonfuls of sugar in it but the milk carton had scarcely been tilted.

"Now this gives one energy," Sister Margaret said happily. "Are these your little girls, Padraic? How pretty they are."

Tabitha and Edith, approaching shyly, were duly introduced. Sister Joan talked about raffia baskets and dried flower posies; Petroc slouched up and volunteered to collect different sorts of rocks from all round the district; the caravan door stayed firmly closed.

"Are your parents around?" Sister Joan enquired of Petroc.

"Mum's gone north and Dad's inside," Petroc said, with no particular emotion.

"My brother," said Padraic sadly, "was framed. An innocent, Sisters. A true innocent, but given to hitting policemen when he's wrongfully accused. It don't do to get on the wrong side of the law. I tell Petroc here that if you get picked up ever you act polite. That's right, ain't it, Sister?"

"Manners maketh man," Sister Joan quoted.

"A rare way of putting it! You hear that, Petroc?" He frowned towards his nephew.

"It wasn't actually my quot—" Sister Joan began.

"Shakespeare," Padraic said. "Lovely way with words that man had. My wife can read that kind of thing something lovely."

"Actually it comes from—" Sister Joan jumped violently as the caravan door was suddenly flung open and a figure wrapped in a brilliantly patterned bedspread swayed on to the threshold, yelling in far from dulcet accents, "Padraic, where the bloody hell are you? My stomach's sticking to my backbone."

"Just seeing to supper, Madge." He had risen to move between the door and the two Sisters. "Five minutes, my sweetheart. Petroc, take the girls over to your place. I'll be along later. I'm terribly sorry, Sisters. I figured as how Madge'd sleep longer, but when the sickness is on her it's not so certain. Reads lovely she does when she's feeling herself. Bit of a comedown for her really, getting wed to a man without education. I tell my girls—I tell them constant—get an education and get a man with education so you won't have cause to feel ashamed."

"I am sure that your girls will grow up to be very proud of their father," Sister Joan said awkwardly.

"Jesus, no!—begging your pardons. I'm reliant on them having better taste than that," Padraic said in alarm. "You'll be wanting Ginny Smith now, I daresay. Last wagon on the right. Nice little woman but she can't cope. Just coming, Madge."

"Wonderful tea." Sister Margaret rose, lifting a hand in farewell as he darted up the steps. "Wonderful man too. Sorely afflicted, which is always a sign of grace."

They walked away, Sister Joan at least being uncomfortably aware of peering eyes, of an old woman smoking a pipe outside her wagon who circled finger and thumb in the ancient sign of protection against the evil eye.

"So interesting to see where they live." Sister Margaret avoided a suspicious looking puddle. "I often feel that Our Dear Lord would have felt very much at home with Romanies. Is this the Smith caravan, Sister?"

"Last in the line. It must be." Sister Joan hesitated as the door opened and a tiny woman came out, peering down at them uncertainly.

"Mrs. Smith? I've come to have a chat about the school project." She raised her voice encouragingly. "Perhaps Conrad or Tabitha told you about it?"

"Conrad did mention—" Mrs. Smith came further down the steps, pulling her dress as straight as crooked seams could make it. "He went over to the village to do some odd jobs for a lady there. The money comes in handy since—my Jeb isn't home yet, you see."

Her Jeb, Sister Joan thought with irritated compassion, was never likely to come home but Ginny Smith evidently believed in keeping up appearances. Theoretically that was, since what could be glimpsed of the interior of the caravan was a jumble of blankets, cushions, soiled underwear strung on a line, and a cat shedding hairs over everything that hadn't been ruined in any other way.

"We're having a school project about this district," Sister Joan said. "Posters and folders and perhaps a school exhibition."

"Well now I don't know—really I don't." Ginny Smith looked more harassed than ever. "With my Jeb not being home and so many chores to do—of course Conrad will be all for it. Bags of energy that lad. Yes, he'll enjoy that—project you said? Hagar too. She needs a hobby does Hagar. Misses her dad, you see. A man about the place makes all the difference, don't you—but then you wouldn't, would you? Being vowed to chastity and all. Will you take a mug of tea?"

She looked round vaguely as if she expected it to materialize out of thin air.

"We'd love to but we really haven't time," Sister Joan said with what she hoped sounded like real regret. "As long as you think the project might be interesting—?"

"Oh, I'm sure. Yes indeed, Sister. I'm afraid everything's a bit untidy right now. I really can't think where Hagar can have got to."

She looked round again as if she expected her daughter to materialize along with the tea.

"As long as we can count on you," Sister Joan said with equal vagueness.

"I was scared you was the attendance man," Ginny Smith confided, coming almost to the bottom of the steps. "Conrad's been coming regular, hasn't he?"

"Yes, very regularly," Sister Joan assured her, "but we shall have to talk some time about his going to the Bodmin School. Petroc will be going there next term so he won't be alone. And Hagar of course is twelve now and also ought to be going into Bodmin."

"I thought as how you wanted to talk about the project," Ginny Smith said.

"Yes, that's the main thing. But the other—"

"I'd not dream of doing anything without my Jeb's approval," the other said firmly. "When he gets home, Sister, then we'll see about Bodmin."

"Yes."

There was no point in arguing, Sister Joan decided. Mrs. Smith was obsessed with the hope that her errant husband would come wandering home, and couldn't be bothered with anything else. It was possible that he might, of course, but if he had any instincts of fastidiousness at all the inside of his caravan would soon send him off again.

"Nice talking to you, Mrs. Smith," she said brightly. "We'd better be going now."

"Yes, well—if you call again my Jeb'll likely be home," Ginny Smith said, with a desperate little clutch at her sagging dress. "Goodnight, Sister." She had turned back up the unpainted wooden steps before there was time for a reply.

"That seems to be that," Sister Joan said.

"Yes indeed." Sister Margaret's round face was shadowed. "How fortunate we are, Sister Joan, not to love where love is not returned. Did you want to see anyone else?"

"That's the lot. I would like to have had a word with Hagar though. She ought to be given a nice, absorbing interest," Sister Joan answered thoughtfully.

"You want no truck with young Hagar. Old Hagar can tell you what you want to know."

The old, pipe smoking woman who had made the sign against the evil eye in their direction had left the steps of her wagon and approached them. Close to she was even older than at first appeared, her face monkey wrinkled,

what showed of her scant hair from beneath the coloured
scarf a dirty white. On her hands a number of very beautiful and incredibly dirty rings gleamed in the setting sun.

"Are you also named Hagar?" Sister Joan asked, resisting the temptation to take a step backwards.

"Hagar Boswell," the old woman nodded. "The Boswells was royalty once—Romany royalty. You heard of
the Boswells?"

"Yes indeed. My name is Sister Joan and this is Sister
Margaret. We are from—"

"I knows where you'm from," the old woman interrupted impatiently. "That convent place where them old
maids is locked up."

"On the contrary we choose the life." Sister Joan
prepared to argue.

"More fools you then," Hagar Boswell said contemptuously. "Young Hagar Smith's off again, preparing herself for a bad end—she's her dad in her that one. Feckless.
We've troubles enough without a couple of nuns bringing
bad luck here. Evil we've got. Evil crawling and creeping."

"Oh, I hardly think so," Sister Margaret began.

"Oh, I hardly think so." The other mocked her in a
high, bitter voice. "Wrapped in cottonwool like babes
come afore their due date you lot be. There's evil here.
Black evil, my fine ladies. If you don't believe me then
walk on to the willows and you'll see."

Muttering angrily she drew her shawl about her and
went off, her scarved head bobbing up and down.

"She is possibly a little touched in the head," Sister
Margaret said in a low voice.

"Possibly." Sister Joan stared after the retreating figure
for a moment, then added, "All the same I think we ought
to stroll on towards the willows."

"To see out evil?" Sister Margaret looked nervous. "Dear Sister Joan, do you think that entirely wise? We are taught that evil seeks us constantly."

"Then perhaps we ought not to flee but turn and face it," Sister Joan said.

"Of course you are right." Sister Margaret looked unhappy. "Or perhaps we may find the poor old lady is a little lacking in her wits. So sweet of her to bless us."

"Bless us?" As they continued their walk Sister Joan looked at her companion in some perplexity.

"That curious gesture she made with finger and thumb—a Roman blessing, I suppose, and all the while being really rather discourteous."

"A Romany blessing—yes," Sister Joan said.

They were approaching the circle of willow trees that screened the pool from any casual glance. The setting sun still made a glory of the sky but their shadows were long and thin behind them on the trampled grass, and the trees seemed to lean together, the young cages of their scarcely leaved branches stark against the landscape. Behind them lights had glowed forth in the windows of several caravans and the smell of cooking had grown stronger.

By mutual consent they had both fallen silent, their shoes quiet on the grass as it grew longer, starred with the pale lace of meadowsweet. At a little distance the splashing of water came to their ears. Sister Joan stepped on to a narrow path that wound down between the willows. At this point the trees were mixed with sturdy oak and ash, the latter trembled slightly as the rising wind caught its silvery leaves.

In the pool two figures were swimming, heads diving down, heels kicking upwards in flashes of spray and bare white skin. The two nuns paused, themselves shielded by the deep gloom cast by the trees, and looked at the scene of sylvan loveliness. The two young creatures in the water dived and broke the surface and dived again, then playfully wrestled like clumsy little bears, then shook water out of their eyes and dived again, becoming on the instant mermaid and merboy with legs straight as arrows and black hair streaming. At the other side of the pool the water shallowed and a rock broke the surface.

Hagar swam to it and mounted the stone, arms raised, ripe young breasts and hips dyed scarlet as the sun dipped lower. Petroc—it was Petroc, she saw—reached the rock and clung to it, head back, childish laughter changing to something else. Something pagan and primitive. Then the moment fled and he gripped her ankles and tumbled her into the water again, the two shapes becoming one as the silver of the pool became darker and was rayed by one beam from the climbing moon.

In complete silence the two nuns turned and walked back to the car, Sister Joan's face dyed with colour. She craved palette and brush and canvas—anything to capture and hold that unearthly loveliness. She also craved oblivion. Of all the companions she might have had then Sister Margaret was the most unsuitable. Sister Margaret had been so innocent and yet she had brought her here. If brandy were needed she rather feared the lay sister would be the one in need of it.

"So wicked," Sister Margaret said, fumbling with the controls of the car once they were safely belted in.

"Perhaps not wicked," Sister Joan said desperately.

"It is a strong word, Sister, and perhaps I am wrong to use it," Sister Margaret said, "but I do feel quite strongly—of course the poor old lady is very likely touched in the head. But how one could so twist the playfulness of those two children—well, words fail me."

At that moment words also failed Sister Joan. She could

only sit staring at her fellow nun's indignant profile as the car leapt forwards.

"You didn't think—?" she said at last.

"Oh, they are not without blame," Sister Margaret said, bumping over the gorse. "The boy was supposed to stay with his cousins while Padraic saw to his poor wife. The habit of strong drink is a curse, Sister. How thankful we must be that we are not afflicted."

"Yes indeed," Sister Joan said automatically.

"The problem is that she is quite well educated," Sister Margaret said. "Padraic is proud of that. He sets great store by education, but there are other things required if one is to be a good wife and mother. On the other hand she has much to try her, poor soul. The law can be quite harsh on men like Padraic and his brother. I do hope they won't catch cold. Not exactly a warm night for swimming."

"And without bathing suits," Sister Joan said dryly.

"It reminded me of Eden," Sister Margaret said wistfully. "Sometimes I wonder what it was like to be there— before the serpent came. Such joy, don't you think? All the garden to play in, and all nature at one's command. And the Father to come for a chat in the cool of the evening. Something wonderful to look forward to every day. Do you want to visit any of the other parents this evening, Sister? The light is almost gone but it would be quite an adventure to drive in the dark."

"I thought we might have another little expedition tomorrow," Sister Joan said.

"Oh, splendid! After Father Malone has heard our confessions? I must clear my conscience before I venture forth again."

"What of?" Sister Joan asked in astonishment.

"My dear, have you forgotten that I broke the grand

silence?'' There was sorrowful reproach in the other's voice. ''Mother Dorothy was so kind about it, even suggesting that I accompany you on this round of visits. One feels like a good stiff penance to redress the balance, don't you think?''

''I suppose.'' Sister Joan felt shame rising.

''And we must both pray for poor old Hagar Boswell. So sad to lose one's wits and see evil where there is only innocence.''

Sister Joan nodded silently. Her conscience—that overactive conscience about which Jacob had so often teased her—was nagging her again. Spiritual pride, she thought uneasily, was probably her besetting sin. She had been so certain that Sister Margaret would be shocked by the unselfconscious nudity, so sure that innocence was generally paired with a narrow mind. Narrow minds were usually dirty minds. She blamed herself for having forgotten that simple fact.

''Anybody for the brandy?'' Sister Perpetua greeted them jokingly as they got out of the car at the back door.

''Everything went very well,'' Sister Margaret said happily. ''You know I believe I am really getting the hang of this driving business. I may ask leave to try out the car in the middle of town very soon.''

''May the saints preserve Bodmin,'' Sister Perpetua said fervently.

''I made a start on supper, Sister.'' Sister Teresa came to the door. ''It won't be as tasty as it usually is, but I thought you might be tired after the driving.''

''Now that is thoughtful of you, Sister.'' Sister Margaret beamed. ''What a lovely treat, to make a pleasant visit and then come home to find one's work done for you. Really, this has been quite a day. And we were given a very stimulating mug of tea too. People are very kind.''

Some of them are, Sister Joan thought, standing stock still. But not all of them, Sister. We have been in the presence of evil tonight and I don't know its source. Not in the old woman or in the kids swimming, but someone. Reaching out to cast a shadow that has no shape. Evil, but I can't put a face to it or a name.

And the bell just then ringing she thrust the certainty to the back of her mind and followed her sisters.

FOUR

✠ ✠ ✠

At school the next day the Romany children had chattered excitedly about "Sister's visit."

"And there was two of them come," Petroc was announcing. "One in a black veil, and Sister Joan in her white. Why's that, Sister?"

"Sister Margaret is a lay sister," she explained. "That means she goes out more into the world than we do. She does the shopping and posts the letters and things like that."

"Then she ain't a proper sister," Billy said firmly.

"Indeed she is." Sister Joan was equally firm. "She keeps the rule just as we all do. In many ways her job is harder because she has more distractions."

"But you come out?" Tabitha said, looking puzzled.

"Only with permission," Sister Joan said.

"What's this rule then?" Conrad enquired.

Sister Joan hesitated. They were about to embark on a geography test and she knew a red herring when she saw one, but on the other hand it was probably wise to tell them something of the life a nun led, to dispel some of the more grotesque misconceptions that got into people's heads.

"When we enter the religious life—become Daughters of Compassion," she said, "we have to train for it, you know, the way one trains for everything. So we spend two years as what is called a postulant—we learn what it means to give up everything for God. Then we take vows that last for one year and after that, if we still want it and if the other sisters agree we take vows that last for the rest of our lives. Vows are promises we make to God."

"What promises, Sister?" This from Samantha Olive who leaned forward, her green eyes alight with interest.

"Poverty—that means not owning things; chastity—that means being pure; obedience—you know what obedience is; and then in our order we take a vow of charity—of love and kindness."

"If you can't own anything, and you can't get wed and you have to do as you're told and go round being nice to everybody it can't be much of a life," Hagar said.

"I think it sounds lovely." Samantha's plain little face was wistful.

"Most of the time it is, but you have to be suited to the life. You have to really want to do it and live it and be it." Sister Joan smiled at her.

"I think I'd rather get married, Sister," Madelyn Penglow said apologetically.

"Getting married is fine too, if you choose the right person. Now, how about that geography test?"

"I've been thinking, Sister," Petroc said sweetly, "that God'd be real upset to see us all inside working on a morning like this. I think He'd say, 'Run out and enjoy yourselves.' "

His black eyes met her own blue ones with a look of

limpid innocence; in his ear the customary gold hoop glinted against black curly hair.

In fewer years than I care to count, Sister Joan thought, with a spasm of amusement, you will be a heartbreaker, my lad.

"The Creator," she said aloud, "has expected people to work ever since they had to leave the garden of Eden. Now Madelyn will give out the papers and Edith will give out the pencils. Some of the questions are going to be too hard for the younger ones. Don't worry about it but do what you can."

The test proceeded smoothly with no more than the normal amount of cheating. She rode back to the convent in the afternoon, her mind reaching ahead to the evening's visits. It was a pity that the other parents would have had warning by now. She had particularly wanted to meet the Olives when they were unaware. Their daughter had an aura about her—not of loneliness. Of apartness. Yes, that was the word. She was set apart in more ways than being a newcomer to the district. The other children who usually teased newcomers for a few days before admitting them into the group had always held aloof from Samantha; yet in some odd fashion they craved her approval, covering up for her when she was, as she frequently was, slow at games, their voices dying into a mumble when Samantha spoke. If it hadn't been a ridiculous notion Sister Joan would have said they were afraid of her.

On Wednesdays Father Malone came to hear confessions and stay on for a bite of tea and a bit of a gossip. The nuns fluttered round him, relishing the only breath of masculinity that entered their lives. Father Malone was elderly and unambitious, unlike his curate Father Stephen who rushed everywhere at top speed as if he were already chasing after a bishop's mitre.

"A very spiritual young priest," old Sister Mary Concepta said in some bewilderment when she had made a confession to him on one occasion, "but a little thoughtless, I fear. He kept asking me what else I had done that was on my conscience, and he didn't seem to understand that being confined to the infirmary with rheumatism doesn't give very many opportunities for occasions of sin."

"Being nearly eighty doesn't make for many opportunities either," Sister Perpetua had boomed. "Man's a young idiot."

"Oh, no, Sister." Sister Mary Concepta's sweet, old face had looked distressed. "He was quite right to press me, but Father Malone makes one feel more comfortable, you know. Always finishes off his visit with a nice little joke. So amusing."

After that, though nothing was said in Sister Joan's hearing, she noticed that Father Malone came nearly always to hear confessions. Not that he was lenient. One was apt to find oneself on one's knees for a good long while after absolution. This Wednesday the fifteen decades of the rosary she had been handed out for penance kept her on her knees for a good three quarters of an hour. She could have saved up the penance for later, but there was no point in doing that with Sister Margaret rooted to the floor in her own place.

By the time they both rose tea was over and Father Malone had driven off in the car that was even more battered than the one into which Sister Margaret now inserted her plump frame.

"All ready, Sister Joan? I can wait while you get a bit of bread and butter from the kitchen," she offered. "It's another fine evening."

"We'll probably be offered a snack," Sister Joan said,

buckling herself in and preparing to hold her heart in her mouth.

It was not only in her mouth but practically jolted through the top of her head by the time Sister Margaret had scraped along the wall and set the vehicle against the wide open gates as if she were ramming the barricades in the French Revolution.

"She's flying like a bird today, isn't she?" she carrolled happily above the screeching of tyres. "Mind you, she usually does when I'm in a good humour."

"Sister, I've never known you in a bad humour," Sister Joan said.

"Oh, I can have my misery moments," her companion insisted, "but a good penance always cheers me up. Isn't it odd that the saying of prayers should be called penance, when the worst penance would be to be forbidden to say any at all? Now where are we off to this evening?"

"The Penglows, the Wesleys and the Holts in that order," Sister Joan said. "Then if we could make a detour on the way home we could call in at the Olives."

"I don't believe that I've heard that name?" Sister Margaret looked enquiring.

"They only arrived in the neighbourhood a couple of months ago. Their daughter, Samantha, joined the school for a term or two before she starts at Bodmin."

"Such a pity that you lose them all to the big schools," Sister Margaret said. "It must be very stimulating to have youngsters about one."

"Also exhausting," Sister Joan said wryly. "The Penglows live on the north ridge."

"I believe that I bought eggs here once when our own chickens refused to lay." Sister Margaret drew up with a triumphant flourish almost level with the white painted gate on the top of which Madelyn and David sat solemnly side by side.

"Good afternoon, Sister." Their mother, trim in a flowered overall, had come out of the house beyond. "I've hot scones and a pot of tea ready. The children were telling me about this project you had in mind, so anything we can do to help—get down and open the gate for the Sisters, children."

Brother and sister solemnly descended and opened the gate. Though they had both obviously been playing out after tea their hands and clothes were spotless. Behind them the house gleamed with fresh white paint and the scent of warm cooking wafted gently from the kitchen as they went in. Sister Joan, while acknowledging the pristine neatness of everyone and everything couldn't help wondering if anything as original as an idea ever penetrated the gleaming heads of the Penglows.

"Now, you just sit down, Sisters, and there'll be tea and hot scones in a jiffy," Mrs. Penglow said. Her voice was quiet and slow. She gave the impression of never hurrying herself for any reason. Sister Joan found it vaguely irritating, but reminded herself that haste didn't mean better—it only meant faster.

"My husband will be in soon, so if you needed to see him—?" their hostess began, bringing in scones and tea.

The room into which she had ushered them was so tidy that anyone else might have suspected that she had actually rushed round to prepare for them but Sister Joan, who had had occasion to visit the house once before when both children came down with light cases of chickenpox, had found the same placid order then.

"There really isn't any need to trouble Mr. Penglow," she said. "The children have told you about the project so there isn't much for me to add, except to enquire if you think you'll be able to help out if necessary. I mean if we have a small exhibition or something of that nature?''

"I can give Madelyn some old Cornish recipes and help her bake a few samples,'' Mrs. Penglow said. "David fancies making a timetable of the local buses—drawing it up neatly with changing prices over the years. His dad will help him with that.''

"But that's a marvellous idea,'' Sister Joan said, with unflattering surprise. "I would like the children to do the bulk of the project themselves, of course.''

"My husband and I will merely lend a helping hand. More scones, Sister?''

Sister Joan hesitated, then declined. The scones were delicious, very light with just the right hint of saltiness, but she resolved on a private penance to remind herself that it was extremely wrong to make superficial snap judgements about people. Underneath their bland, conventional exterior the Penglows were probably seething with originality. Sister Margaret, who never made judgements, had accepted a second scone with a clear conscience and was gazing about the trim, bright room with an expression of happy approval.

"Getting on all right at school, are they?'' Mrs. Penglow allowed a faintly anxious frown to cross her smooth brow. It was obvious that she had no real qualms about her offspring. They would turn out as perfectly as her scones and the homemade bilberry jam she was now pressing upon Sister Margaret.

"Very nicely. When they go to the senior school they ought to get on very well,'' Sister Joan said. She had planned to mention that it might not be a bad thing for brother and sister to be put in different classes so that each might develop a more independent personality, but such a suggestion wouldn't have achieved any result. In the end they would turn out to be mirror images of their parents, a thought that depressed her for no coherent reason.

They rose to leave when Sister Margaret had wistfully but heroically refused a third scone. Mr. Penglow, driving up as they reached the gate, saluted them with the slightly formal politeness of a non-Catholic who isn't absolutely sure he likes nuns cluttering up the threshold.

"Such lovely scones." Sister Margaret let in the clutch with a triumphant grinding sound. "Do you think it would have been very bold of me to ask for the recipe?"

"I think she'd have been flattered," Sister Joan reassured her. "I'll ask Madelyn to get it from her mother, if you like."

"That would be very kind. Such a treat for us all to have on Sunday. Did you say Wesleys next?"

"Please, Sister—though I've a feeling that nobody will be in. The Wesleys are rumoured to be allergic to any notions of anything resembling work, and I'm afraid Billy is dedicated to keeping up the family reputation."

In that prophesy she was proved right. When they drew up outside the cottages where the Wesleys lived they were greeted by a neighbour hanging over her gate and calling that everybody at Number Six was out.

"Gone to the pictures in Bodmin. It's *Rambo*," she informed them.

"Rambo must mean good, I suppose," Sister Margaret said, backing up the street. "I never can keep up with current idioms."

"I think it's the name of the film, Sister. It's a series that's popular."

"Like the Doris Day films," Sister Margaret said. "I saw all the reissues. Most enjoyable. Did you say the Holts next?"

"The big farm over towards Druid's Way. The Olives

live about a mile further on, so we can cut back across the greenway if that suits you, Sister?''

"Sounds splendid. I so seldom get the chance to drive up to the greenway," Sister Margaret said happily. "There are no shops up there and no excuse to go, but all that level ground would give one a wonderful chance to drive fast without worrying whether or not one was going to hit something."

Sister Joan, feeling slight surprise that her companion did actually fret a little about the safety of her driving, said nothing but reminded herself to tighten her seat belt when the visit to the Holts was over.

Timothy, as she had guessed, was with his father, the two of them emerging from a barn as the nuns stopped the car and approached the house.

" 'Evening to you, ladies. Tim said you'd be calling and staying for a bite of supper, I hope? The wife makes a tasty fish pie."

"Oh, I do hope she will give me the recipe," Sister Margaret whispered as they went into the big house where a comfortable shabbiness prevailed and Mrs. Holt, her hair scraped back from an unexpectedly pretty face, waited to greet them.

"Nice to see you, Sister Joan." She shook hands heartily. "Sister—Margaret? We have passed briefly once or twice out shopping. Tim, go and wash your hands. That lad'd spend his entire life mucking out if he wasn't chided. Supper's ready and there's plenty for guests so I'll not take a refusal. This project now—it sounds like a very good idea, doesn't it, William? It might focus attention on the way people do actually live out here—not all farmers are millionaires, not by any means. You'll not object to the telly being on. We're following a serial—I'll fill you in on what you've missed but first I'll dish up. Stargazy pie and apples and ice-cream to follow. And plenty of seconds. Tim, will you get your hands washed? That boy is never happier than when he's grubbing in the soil or scratching the pigs' backs or doing something that's sure to make work for me.''

There was no doubt, thought Sister Joan as she was bustled to a long table groaning with food, that Mrs. Holt could talk Sister Gabrielle off her feet any time. Despite the array of food, the cheerfulness, the air of having a big family to look after, she was aware that Mrs. Holt's manner covered past heartbreaks—three babies in the local cemetery before Tim had survived, and two miscarriages afterwards. Her chatter was her way of dealing with grief, her constant stream of grumbles her way of hiding the intense protective love with which she regarded her son.

''Well, now this is a rare treat.'' Mr. Holt, as big and ungainly a man as his son was a boy, took his place at the table. ''It's not often we get the Sisters over, is it, love? And Tim's doing all right at the school, is he? Got a good head on his shoulders that lad—when my time comes I'll be leaving the farm in good hands. Now, who's for a bit of pie?''

''William.'' His wife was scarlet. ''We've not said grace yet.''

''We never—oh, yes, of course.'' Mr. Holt who was not a Catholic put down the serving spoon and looked rather at a loss.

''Bless this food to our use and us to Thy service,'' Sister Joan said, ''and keep all safe here and everywhere. Amen.''

Mother and son crossed themselves in unison with the Sisters and Mr. Holt picked up the serving spoon again and plunged into the fluffy potato crust with an air of relief.

The conversation centred on the intended project, Timothy volunteering several bright ideas of his own. When he made them his parents listened avidly, Mrs. Holt exclaiming softly under her breath, "Well, the lad has a point there, I must say. Yes, indeed."

It was surprising, in view of the way they felt about him, that he was turning out to be such a nice boy, Sister Joan thought. She had no doubt that the farm would be in good hands one day.

"Not another bite, honestly." She put up her hand as Mrs. Holt started passing out tarts with a bowl of ice-cream. "I am full of your marvellous pie. Sister Margaret won't be happy until she has coaxed the recipe out of you, Mrs. Holt."

"Oh, it'd be a pleasure, Sister," their hostess said promptly. "The secret's in the marinade—lemon juice with a touch of sugar. It gives the fish just that touch of flavour."

"Ah, that explains it then," Sister Margaret said. "Very subtle amounts I think, but you were going to watch your serial. I'd not wish to spoil your enjoyment."

"There's a repeat on Saturday," Mrs. Holt said. "Tim'll watch it though while I show you how I make the dish."

Timothy, with a muttered apology, slid thankfully from the table and bolted into an alcove where a large television set was enthroned rather like a monarch on his throne.

Sister Joan, setting her empty cup back in its saucer, looked up to meet Mr. Holt's steady regard.

"We've a new calf, Sister Joan, if you've a mind to see." He spoke gruffly, giving a little jerk of his head towards the door.

"Well I don't—yes, I should like to see it very much," Sister Joan said, impelled to acceptance by something unspoken at the back of his mild grey eyes. They walked across the darkening yard towards the barn, he pausing to take a lantern from a hook on the wall as they reached the barn.

"Animals prefer the softer light. I find they give richer milk if they're not always in glare."

He lit it neatly with his big, calloused hands and they passed on into a high, vaulted place with the smell of milk, and straw and the unmistakable smell of birth.

"Dropped her calf two nights since. Nice little thing. I've a fondness for small creatures—why I've held out against factory methods, I suppose. Not that I'm sentimental, and there's nothing like a good steak but at least give the creatures the chance to see a bit of sky first, eh, Sister?"

"I'm sure you're right, Mr. Holt." Sister Joan moved to the rail of the stall and looked at the long-legged, large-headed baby, now suckling contentedly. The mother turned a larger head, curiosity in the brown eyes, but seeing or smelling the human she knew lost interest.

"She'm a good old maid," Mr. Holt said, dropping the standard English he had been speaking for a moment, as he leaned to scratch the cow's rump. "Why did you really come here this evening, Sister?"

"To talk about the project," Sister Joan said. "You know, being a nun it is often difficult for me to get out to meet the parents of my pupils as often as I'd like. I hope you don't—"

"Mind you coming? Glad of it. Never had any particular faith myself but the wife sets store by her church and I'd no objection to having Tim reared in the same faith. Point is, Sister, I know that prayer you said before we ate and there's nothing in it about keeping folks safe. I thought as how you were hinting that you wanted a private word, like.''

''No, honestly, I wasn't. I don't know why I put that in,'' Sister Joan said, feeling suddenly foolish. ''It was an impulse.''

''A good one I'm thinking.'' Mr. Holt drew back from the cow and frowned down at his smaller companion. ''I thought as how you might have picked up the scent that's been in my nostrils these past weeks.''

''Scent?''

''Evil,'' said Mr. Holt flatly and smote his hands lightly against the rail to emphasize his point. ''That's an unfashionable word, isn't it? Well, I'm not a clever bloke—all I know's farming, but I know evil too. It's around, Sister. I can smell it on the wind, but I can't tell you where it is or the way it's coming. I can only tell you that it is coming. I've no enemies that I know, but evil takes no count of that. And I tell you frankly, Sister, that if anything harmed the wife or my lad—''

''Mr. Holt?'' She stared at the big, clenching hands.

''I'd kill,'' he said with a terrible simplicity. ''I'd kill, Sister. Shall we go in?''

Lifting up the lantern again he stood aside politely to let her pass out of the barn.

FIVE

✠ ✠ ✠

"You added something to the Grace this evening," Sister Margaret remarked when they were back in the car. "A very kind thought, Sister. It's clear they dote on that boy."

She turned to wave to the trio standing at the door as they drove away. The recipe for stargazy pie reposed in her bag and her face was irradiated with quiet content. Not for one second had Sister Margaret been aware of the creeping presence of anything.

"You should have come to look at the new calf, Sister," Sister Joan said. "It was so sweet."

"I'm afraid that I always get a guilty feeling before anything else when I see small creatures," Sister Margaret said. "Before I entered the religious life I was quite partial to the occasional lamb chop. Even now I do occasionally wonder if we ought to eat fish, but then I read an article once that said lettuces scream and eggs faint when you start preparing them. So I reckon we have to eat something."

They had turned on to the track that ran towards the area of the moors known locally as the greenway, an area where bracken and ling gave way to deep, soft earth and a natural windbreak formed by a deep and wide dip in the landscape through which ribbons of tiny streamlets watered the fertile ground. The light had quite faded, but the scent of wild verbena drifted through the open window of the car.

"Is that where the Olives live?" Sister Margaret gestured ahead to a dark bulk set back from the flowering grass. "It's the old Druid place, surely? That was before your time, dear, but a brother and sister owned the place. Quite reclusive in their ways, so it was generally rumoured they were exceedingly rich, and a nephew—or was it a niece? I forget which and it really doesn't matter— he or she started coming over to visit the couple, hoping for something, I daresay, but when they died—influenza, the virulent kind—they found out there was no money at all. The place stood empty for years and then the niece— or was it nephew?—sold it and it's passed through a series of owners since. Funny, but despite the land being so fertile and rich nobody's actually got down and cultivated it properly. But it's a beautiful spot, and it is rather refreshing to see somewhere that hasn't been tamed for commercial purposes."

It looked lonely, Sister Joan thought, as they stopped the car—Sister Margaret having heroically refrained from speeding along the deserted track—and walked up to the sprawling mass of stone with its Victorian additions in the shape of cupola and turrets outlined against the evening sky. The black stone loomed against the dark night and the square of light in the windows did nothing to dispel the sudden and disturbing impression that the house crouched on the flowerstrewn moor like some wild beast waiting to spring.

She frowned impatiently at her own foolishness, deciding that while a vivid imagination was all very well in an artist it was out of place in a woman vowed to the religious life. And the impression had been erroneous anyway, since the main door opened as they neared it and a flood of cheerful light illumined Samantha's small frame.

"Do come in, Sister. I was afraid that you weren't going to come," she invited.

"I hope we're not too late. This is Samantha, Sister. Sister Margaret is lay sister at the convent."

By the time she had finished the introduction they were in a square, panelled hall and Mrs. Olive, her slender figure enhanced by tight black trousers and a white shirt, was on her way down the stairs with outstretched hand and a manner very different from her previous languid one when she had first brought her daughter to the school.

"Sister Joan, how pleasant to see you again. Sister Margaret, how do you do? I was beginning to think that Samantha had got hold of the wrong end of the stick but she insisted that you'd be coming."

"Only a brief visit, I'm afraid." Sister Joan glanced at the small steel fob watch pinned to her belt. "We had other parents to see and overstayed our welcome."

"Oh, surely not. I can't imagine your outstaying your welcome anywhere. Come into the warmth and sit down."

The long drawing-room was warmer than would have been comfortable in the depths of winter. Both the nuns flinched slightly as they were met by a blast of hot air from every direction at once. Not only central heating warmed the room but a huge fire burned in the cavernous fireplace above which a large photograph of Samantha, taken some years before, smiled coyly down, clutching a pink rabbit.

"Coffee? Tea? I don't suppose that I dare offer you a cocktail?" She moved to a smart cabinet that looked small and incongruous against the faded grandeur of the room.

"The point is that we wouldn't dare accept it," Sister Joan said lightly. "All I came about was to enquire if we can ask for your co-operation in the matter of the school project."

"It's a local project, isn't it?" Mrs. Olive looked politely attentive. "Naturally my husband and I will give all the help we can, but as newcomers there isn't very much we can add to the knowledge that people already have. We're still finding our way round ourselves, you see. But if it's a question of money—"

"No, it really isn't." Sister Joan felt the familiar blush of shame at the realization that most people associated nuns with collecting boxes.

"Then I really don't—my husband is fond of photography. He could take some photographs of local beauty spots, I suppose. He took that one of Samantha on her fifth birthday. We've always loved it."

"If the parents actually do the project it won't be the children's work," Sister Joan said. "I was hoping that we might have an open day at the school—invite people to come and see what the pupils themselves have produced."

"It sounds very exciting, don't you think so, Samantha darling?" The green eyes, so like the child's save that they looked out between heavily mascara'd lashes, turned to where Samantha stood.

"Yes." A flat monosyllable devoid of expression. Samantha's lively welcome had flared and died.

"Perhaps a folder about this house with drawings? I believe it's quite an old building?" Sister Joan suggested.

"Now that's a splendid idea," Mrs. Olive said. "The house is eighteenth century, I believe. My husband is very keen on that period. He's writing a book set in the—oh, darling, I was just about to boast of you."

She had turned as a man entered the room.

"Then it's fortunate that I came in to put an end to it," he said, advancing with outstretched hands to where the visitors still stood. "I'm Clive Olive, Samantha's father. You will be Sister Joan and—?"

"Sister Margaret. How do you do?"

"As well as can be expected." He glanced down with raised eyebrows.

Sister Joan, following his glance, found herself staring at a built-up shoe. A club foot? An accident?

"Sit down, won't you?" He nodded towards the armchairs scattered about the room. "Has anyone offered you anything yet?"

"We did, Daddy, but they have to go," Samantha said.

"But you will come again?" His thin, clever face had bright, squirrel eyes. The greyish hair that grew thickly on the long head had the aspect of a squirrel's pelt.

"If we need help with the project," Sister Joan said. "As I was explaining to your wife the idea is for the children to produce work that can be mounted in a small school exhibition. Nothing very elaborate."

"It sounds charming." The squirrel eyes moved slowly over her. "Doesn't it sound charming, Julia?"

"We'll certainly give Samantha all the encouragement we can," his wife said.

"Fine. Then we won't detain you any longer." Sister Joan turned away slightly from the probing, stripping gaze. "Samantha seems to be settling down in school very well."

Nobody had asked but she thought she might as well throw in the information.

"Samantha is infinitely adaptable," her father said. "Aren't you, darling?"

"Yes, well—thank you again," Sister Joan said, wondering what exactly she was thanking them for. "Sister Margaret?"

"Good evening." Sister Margaret, who had stood dumbly, gazing round, came to life again.

"I'll see you out." Mrs. Olive moved, thin and graceful, to the door.

At the back of the hall a long passage stretched past the wide staircase, presumably to the kitchen quarters. Sister Joan, glancing back, saw someone standing there. She caught a glimpse of hair so fair that it looked almost white, a classical profile, a lean, athletic body clad in jeans and sweatshirt. Then Mrs. Olive turned her sleek head, saying in a raised voice, "In a moment, Jan."

A side door was opened and closed. The nuns came out to the front step.

"Au pairs can get so bored in the country when there isn't anywhere to go," Mrs. Olive said deprecatingly.

"But I thought—I assumed that your au pair was a girl," Sister Joan said.

"Oh, Kiki got bored too and left us. Jan was recommended through the same agency so I'm hoping that the same pattern won't repeat itself," Mrs. Olive said.

"Through a local agency?" Sister Joan asked.

"One in Bodmin—Foreign Companion Helps—something like that. So far he seems to be settling down, but one can never tell."

The car that picked up Samantha from school always stopped at some distance. She had never bothered to look closely at who was driving it. Not that it was any of her business if the Olives chose to fill their house with male au pairs. Handsome male au pairs, Sister Joan amended, and rebuked herself for being narrow minded.

"Next time you must stay longer," Julia Olive said. The languidness was back in her voice.

"It would be most interesting to see something of such an old house," Sister Joan agreed.

"Most of it is in very bad repair," Mrs. Olive told her. "The basement is very damp and the foundations quite unstable. It will require a lot of work on it before it can be put right, I'm afraid. Good evening again, Sisters." Without waiting to see them into the car she turned and went back into the house.

"We shall have to hurry or we'll be late for chapel," Sister Joan said. "We've missed recreation already."

"So we have." Sister Margaret gave herself a little shake and got hastily into the car.

"You were very quiet in there, Sister. Was anything wrong?" Sister Joan glanced at her companion as the latter started the engine.

"I was looking at the dirt," Sister Margaret said, "and wishing that I had a bucket of hot soapy water and a scrubbing brush. Of course one cannot blame the poor lady. It is an enormous house to clean."

"It didn't strike me as particularly dirty," Sister Joan said, puzzled. "A bit faded and some of the furniture didn't suit the room too well, but hardly dirty."

"Very dirty," said Sister Margaret with unusual firmness and gripped the wheel as the engine sprang into life.

Whatever occupied her mind had at least emptied it of the desire to break speed records, Sister Joan reflected, as they rode home at a moderate speed. Her own mind was a ragbag of impressions which she would have to sort out later.

"I'll put the car away, Sister. You hurry on into chapel," Sister Margaret said as they swept up to the convent.

Chapel, Sister Joan thought, is exactly what I need. This round of visits has muddled me terribly.

She walked briskly to the side door and let herself in, the thought crossing her mind that the habit of leaving the door open was not perhaps a very wise one. Anyone from the laity who wanted to pray in the middle of the night was scarcely likely to come all the way out to the convent in order to gratify their wish. On the other hand a thief or a prowler could easily get in. It might do no harm to have a quiet word with Mother Dorothy on the subject.

"Oh, there you are, Sister! Did you have a pleasant evening? Pleasanter than mine, I'm sure."

Sister David, snub nose twitching violently as was her habit when agitated, met her at the door of the chapel.

"Is something wrong, Sister?"

"The holy water in the stoup has all dried up," Sister David said plaintively. "It is always refilled on Wednesdays as you know and now there isn't a drop left. I can't for the life of me understand it. I checked the stoup for cracks but there aren't any, and in any case the floor would have been wet had it leaked. It looks as if someone actually drank it all up and that's too ridiculous to contemplate."

"What have you done about it?"

"Fortunately there is sufficient for the blessing and tomorrow morning we must ask Sister Margaret to take the water cans over to Father Malone so that he can bless them as soon as they're filled. I did suggest to Mother that we telephone and ask Father to come here for the blessing, but she said we couldn't expect him to come rushing backwards and forwards when we were the ones who had been careless—but I am certain that I was not careless, Sister. The stoup was full otherwise I would naturally have asked Father to bless the next batch of water after he had heard confessions this afternoon."

Little Sister David sounded near to tears.

"I'm sure it will be sorted out," Sister Joan said warmly, wishing she was as sure as she sounded, and went on into the chapel, sliding to her knees with a sense of relief.

Prayers and the nightly blessing that immediately preceded the grand silence were effective barriers against discussing the matter further that night. She put the other questions firmly into the storage cupboard at the back of her mind and concentrated on her Maker.

Morning brought a light shower of rain that was refreshing to the spirits even though it meant she would have to don the unwieldy gaberdine over her habit to protect herself against a wetting. When she went out to the back to saddle up Lilith she bumped into Sister Margaret who looked less than her normal cheerful self.

"Mother Dorothy has told me to go to the presbytery with the water cans so that Father can bless a new batch of holy water," she said. "It seems there isn't any left, which seems quite extraordinary to me. I do so dislike driving in the rain. Lampposts are apt to leap up at one, you know, and the car skids on the wet track."

"Wait until it clears up. It is only a light shower," Sister Joan suggested.

"One hopes so, which is a very ungrateful thing to say," the other replied, "seeing that without rain the flowers wouldn't grow. But it is terribly bad for poor Sister Mary Concepta's rheumatism, and the worst of it is that she never complains. I can feel every twinge of her pain in my own joints—oh, what a grumbler I sound today! You must forgive me, Sister. This is poor thanks for the delightful visits we have paid."

"You probably got out of bed the wrong side this morning. I know that I did."

"I'm sure you're right. Gadding about isn't conducive

to a quiet mind, is it? Well, as I have to drive into town at least I can get some more of Sister Mary Concepta's embrocation at the same time. Have a pleasant day, Sister.''

Something, thought Sister Joan, saddling the horse and mounting up, had ruffled the clear stream of the lay sister's spirits. Surely not the weather or the unaccustomed visiting? Perhaps the evil that William Holt had so startlingly mentioned had reached out to affect even Sister's tranquil spirit. She wished that her former prioress were here. Mother Agnes with her El Greco profile, her air of timeless aristocracy, had understood subtleties, half-formed fears, uncertainties in a way that the brisk Mother Dorothy could not. For the latter there were no greys, no shadows, only plain black and white. She was perfect when it was a matter of dealing with would-be saints in the postulancy or a nun uncertain of a particular aspect of the rule, but she couldn't deal with spiritual cobwebs.

Once riding across the moor her spirits lifted even though the rain was becoming heavier. The air up here was clean and sharp and heathery and the faint pain that had been gripping her temples when she awoke was lifted. This morning there would probably be absentees. Contrary to popular belief the Romanies hated rain, huddling like cats in their wagons when it was wet. For the children who did turn up she would light the old-fashioned oil stove in the corner of the classroom and brew up hot soup.

As she had expected none of the Romanies were there. The Penglows were, clad in identical mackintoshes and sou'westers and conscientiously scraping their shoes on the iron mat outside the door; Billy Wesley arrived in the pick-up with Mr. Holt and Timothy; the car dropped Samantha closer to the school than usual and sped off, the beautiful young man at the wheel. Considering the weather fifty percent attendance was excellent.

Having only half the school present also meant they could pull their chairs into a semicircle around the glowing stove while she abandoned the formal curriculum in favour of story-telling, first relating the Hans Christian Anderson story of the Ugly Duckling and then inviting the children to make their own contributions.

"I know Cinderella," Madelyn volunteered, after some prompting from her brother.

"Fine. You tell it then." Sister Joan frowned at Billy Wesley who had audibly groaned and rolled his eyes up to heaven.

Madelyn, with David supplying at least half the narrative, launched into a long and meticulous and infinitely boring retelling of the old tale. Sister Joan allowed her mind to wander.

Someone—and she doubted if it was one of the nuns unless someone was quietly going mad without anybody else noticing—someone was helping themselves fairly liberally to candles, flowers and holy water from the chapel. All those things were readily available elsewhere, but would not of course be blessed. Someone needed candles, flowers and water that had been blessed. Why?

The big crucifix had been removed from the altar and put back again within a few minutes. She cast her mind back to the sequence of events. She had gone to the chapel and found the altar bare save of candlesticks. She had hurried into the hall and stood there, debating with herself whether or not to interrupt Mother Dorothy's session with the postulants. Then she had returned to the chapel and seen the crucifix back in its place. Either the thief had found it was too heavy to steal or—or the thief hadn't been a thief at all, merely someone who had wanted her to notice the crucifix was missing.

In that case they must have been hiding nearby. The

confessional. That box with its closed door, its secret darkness where sins were whispered into Father Malone's ear every Wednesday afternoon—that would have held person and crucifix. She hadn't stopped to search.

"And they lived happy after ever," Madelyn said.

"Thank you, Madelyn. That was very nice," Sister Joan said, pulling her mind back. "Now who is going to be next?" She smiled round expectantly.

The others looked at one another.

"I know about Robin Hood," Billy said unexpectedly.

"Good. You tell us the story about him then."

"He lived in Sherwood Forest and he took things from the poor—no, that's wrong. He took things from the rich and give 'em to the poor and everybody loved him very much, except the Sheriff of Nottingham but he went out and stuck a sword through the Sheriff of Nottingham and then pricked him all over with arrows and then cut off his head," Billy said with relish.

"That's a horrid story, isn't it, Sister?" Samantha said primly.

"No, it's jolly good," Timothy began and stopped dead, uncertainty in his face. After a moment he said lamely, "I guess it is horrid too, more horrid than good."

"Do you know a story, Samantha?" Sister Joan asked.

"There was once a lady and a gentleman and they got married and had a little baby girl and lived in a very nice house and lived happily afterwards until they were all a hundred years old and then they all went straight to Heaven," Samantha said.

"What happened to them before they went to Heaven?" Billy enquired.

"Nothing," said Samantha serenely. "Nothing ever happened to them at all."

"Wasn't that a bit dull for them?" Sister Joan asked cautiously.

"Oh, no, Sister, it was just lovely!" The child's green eyes blazed suddenly, lighting up the plain, pale little face. "It was just lovely."

"I think that was a very nice story," Madelyn said.

"Yes, but—" Sister Joan broke off at the sound of an approaching lorry. "Excuse me for a few moments, children. I think the others may have arrived."

When she went out to the front, however, where the drizzling rain had lessened to a wet mist hanging on the air, only Padraic Lee alighted, jumping down from the driver's seat and squelching towards her through the wet grass.

"Good morning, Sister. Sorry to interrupt but I was wondering if Petroc had turned up at school," he greeted her.

"None of the Romany children are here. You should know since you drive them."

"It was raining." He gave her a reproachful look.

"The children won't melt in the rain," she said irritably, aware of a nasty, sinking feeling at the pit of her stomach. "And Petroc isn't here."

"Then I reckon he's nipped off to try and see his dad," Padraic said. "Funny though, not to leave word with someone. He knows that I'd try to argue him out of it but I'd never stop him if he'd fixed his mind."

"Mr. Lee, your nephew is twelve years old," she reminded him. "He's a child. You can't let children do whatever they fix their minds on."

"Petroc's a sensible lad," his uncle argued. "I didn't take much note last night when I went by his wagon and he wasn't there. I figured he'd gone off to do a bit of—"

"Poaching," Sister Joan said severely.

''Nature watching,'' he substituted with a grin. ''Any-ways this morning seeing it was wet and all was peaceful-like, I figured we'd sleep in and I let him be, but then I minded myself that I'd some scrap to pick up in Bodmin so I went over to see if he'd a fancy to come and he wasn't there. Bunk not slept in. So I wondered if he'd hightailed it over to school.''

''None of your children came this morning,'' Sister Joan said. ''Mr. Lee, if Petroc is missing shouldn't you get the police?''

It was, of course, entirely the wrong suggestion. She knew it even before his face closed against the idea of authority and he said defensively, ''No need to bring the law in on this, Sister. Before you know it we'll have them social workers down about our necks like fleas. My good lady would be very upset about that.''

Sister Joan doubted if his ''good lady'' would recognize either policeman or social worker through the alcoholic haze in which she dwelt but it would have been unkind to say so. Instead she said, ''Has Petroc ever done this be-fore?''

''Not stayed away all night, Sister. He likes his bed that lad and it came on to rain around midnight, so he'd have come home for sure.''

''Have you asked around the camp?—yes, of course you'll have done that. Had he taken anything with him?''

''I had a quick look round, but I couldn't see anything gone though I didn't look close.''

''Had he money on him?''

''A couple of pounds. Never any more.''

''That wouldn't get him very far on a train or bus,'' she began but he interrupted, ''He wouldn't go that way, Sis-ter. He'd likely walk until he could pick up a hitch.''

''But surely that's terribly dangerous?''

"Suicidal these days with all the rogues and criminals about," he agreed, "and Petroc knows enough not to do it. But he were that upset about his dad being framed though he never let on—has his pride that lad. But he might have took it into his head."

"If you will wait a few moments, Mr. Lee, I'll ask the children."

Going back inside she met a curious gaze of five pairs of eyes.

"Aren't the others coming, Sister?" Timothy enquired.

"Not today. Children, have any of you seen Petroc since last evening? He seems to be missing."

Five heads hesitated and then were shaken.

"Has he been stolen away?" Madelyn asked, her blue eyes round.

"No, of course not. He's simply run off for a piece of mischief, just to be naughty," Sister Joan said. "He'll turn up later, I'm sure."

"Who'd want to steal Petroc away anyhow?" Billy asked scornfully. "He's just a gyppo."

"A Romany boy," Sister Joan corrected, "and one who pays more attention to his lessons than you do, Billy Wesley. Look, if you have seen him then it would be much better if you said."

"But we haven't," David said stolidly. "Dad and Mum won't let Madelyn and me go near the Romany camp, and you were in our house yourself last evening, Sister Joan. We were both there."

"I was out at the pictures," Billy said, adding hastily as Sister Joan's eye fell on him, "and I didn't see him. You can ask my mum."

"Thank you, children." Sister Joan turned and went out again to where Padraic Lee waited, shifting from one leg to the other and scowling at the sky as if he dared it to rain on him.

"No luck?" He gave her an anxious look.

"The children haven't seen anything of him, and I was in most of their homes last evening," she answered, "so it's pretty certain they don't know. Mr. Lee, I know you have to collect scrap from Bodmin but in view of what's happened I think I'll close school for today. The trouble is that I don't have a telephone and I can't put them all on Lilith's back and take them to their respective homes."

"I'll drop them off for you, Sister, and then drive into Bodmin and make a few enquiries same time as I'm picking up the scrap," Padraic said obligingly.

"That would be very kind of you, Mr. Lee. I am truly grateful. Children! Children, get your boots and coats on quickly. I've decided to give you a holiday."

Raising her voice cheerfully she went back to her pupils, aware that she was suddenly in the grip of one of those impulses to action that occasionally gripped her.

"It's because Petroc isn't here, isn't it, Sister?" Madelyn's rosy face was troubled.

"That and the rain. Your parents will be in?"

There were murmurs of assent.

Drawing on her neat white plastic mackintosh and tying her hair back under its hood, Samantha said thoughtfully, as if she were testing a new idea in her mind, "He went away just like Kiki did. Vanished, just like her. Isn't it funny, Sister?"

SIX

✠ ✠ ✠

The temptation to rush off in several directions at once was strong. Sister Joan resisted it, helped Padraic to cram the children into the front of his small lorry, and went back into the school to damp down the fire in the stove and put the chairs back into place. These practical actions kept at bay a fear that had started in the pit of her stomach and was threatening to spread. Normally the absence of one of the Romany children would have occasioned in her nothing worse than irritation since it meant someone would have fallen behind the others when they returned to the class. But this was different. The feeling that it might be the culmination of all the small puzzling incidents that had recently occurred gripped her mind and refused to be silenced.

At least she had most of the day left before she was due to return to the convent. That, having dismissed her pupils, she might be expected to return immediately was a consideration she did succeed in putting aside. There was nothing in the rule that stated she must return at once if, for any reason, school closed early.

"Remember always," Mother Agnes had cautioned,

"that to obey the letter of the rule while ignoring the inner spirit that gives it coherence is as bad as downright disobedience. Poverty does not mean only relinquishing material possessions. It means an emptying of the self that the Divine may enter and make us richer than any millionaire who has only material possessions to shield him against the dark. Obedience is never a slavish following of the rule. It is making the rule part of oneself so that if all writings were lost they could be rewritten simply by watching your behaviour."

And what does one do, Sister Joan enquired in her mind of her former prioress, when obeying the spirit of the rule might lead to an injustice, to a lack of charity?

Charity must come before everything, Mother Agnes replied—or perhaps it was only her own mind making noises.

She locked the door and brought Lilith out of the shed. The rain was still a fine mist on the morning air, but there were flashes of sunlight that coloured the drops of water hanging on the grasses, and the wind had the fugitive sweetness of spring.

And please God, let Petroc Lee be sitting contrite in his wagon when I get to the Romany camp, she prayed silently, mounting up.

With the ceasing of the rain the camp had come to life, windows being opened, the inevitable smell of cooking already drifting over the trampled ground. There was no sign of Tabitha or Edith but Conrad walked to meet her, his broad face sullen.

"I was going to come to school but Padraic was looking for Petroc and there wasn't no transport," he began defensively.

"School's closed for the day anyway. Has Mr. Lee been

back here?'' She slid to the ground, wishing the promised jeans had materialized.

''He took Tabby and Edie off with him. Me and Hagar are supposed to stay here in case Petroc comes back.''

''When did you see Petroc last?'' Looping the reins over her arm she began to stroll towards the Lee wagon, keeping her tone casual.

''After school yesterday. He went off somewhere.''

''Did he say where he was going?''

''I didn't ask, did I? He just went off and I stayed around, helping Mum tidy the wagon.''

''So you were here all evening?''

''Most of it. I might have taken a bit of a walk.''

''By yourself?'' Sister Joan looked her surprise.

''Hagar and me went for a bit of a walk. We was arguing.''

''Oh?'' Sister Joan gave him an enquiring look.

''The point is that it's not fair, not fair at all, that I help Mum and do an evening job three times a week while Hagar sits on her ass—sorry, Sister, while Hagar never washes a cup. She's twelve and a girl and she ought to help out.''

''Indeed she ought and it is very good of you to do so,'' Sister Joan said warmly.

''Well, it ain't appreciated,'' Conrad said, pronouncing the word with a kind of gloomy pride. ''I'm thirteen and a man and I ought not to be doing female jobs. I've got to be the man of the house now that Dad's run off, and I can't do everything.''

''So you told your sister that she ought to be doing more to help. What did Hagar say?''

''She argued,'' Conrad said. ''She thinks she's going to be a model or something daft like that. I told her she'd end up *mochte*.''

He used the Romany word for dirty with great vigour. Sister Joan who had hopefully read a book about the Romany tongue with some idea of getting closer to the children looked at him thoughtfully. She had abandoned the idea when she realized that everybody spoke English anyway, but she had noticed that in moments of stress they came out with the ancient words.

"Where's Hagar now?" she asked.

"Gone shopping with Mum. Mum took her part in the end. Said Hagar might go far because she's so pretty. A pair of twerps both of them."

"Not a very respectful way to talk about your mother," Sister Joan said mildly. "Do you think anyone would mind if I took a look inside Petroc's wagon? He might have left a clue."

"You're not working for the police, are you?" Conrad looked at her suspiciously.

"No, of course not. I'm just here to help." She spoke reassuringly and, after a few seconds, he nodded.

"Over there. It ain't locked. I'll wait outside."

Inside everything was neat, shabby and reasonably clean. Evidently Padraic took care of his nephew as well as his own small daughters. There was a hooked rag rug on the floor and a coloured poster of the Princess of Wales on the wall alongside a mirror and a clumsily embroidered text that stated confidently, "God is Love." The double bed had been neatly made as had the low bunk pushed beneath it, and there were dishes in a draining rack on a plastic tray. Garments were hung on a steel frame and bulged out of two large plastic bags. She pulled them out and went through them swiftly but there was nothing to give the smallest clue except for a leather money box stuffed in the bottom of one bag. When she took it it rattled and from its weight she guessed it to be almost full. If Petroc had been running off to try to see his father surely he'd have taken his money with him.

Pushing money box and garments back in the bags she stood up and looked round in some perplexity. There was absolutely nothing here to suggest that Petroc hadn't simply gone off for a ramble. Gone off and not yet returned.

When she came outside again she stood for a moment, watching the other members of the camp as they moved about their daily chores, women pegging out washing with anxious glances skyward, a small group of men lifting pieces of scrap iron on to a pick-up truck. A twelve-year-old boy was missing and nobody seemed to care. By now they ought to have organized a search party.

"You'm finished poking and prying then?"

Old Hagar had approached, black eyes inimical, finger and thumb rounded in the sign against the evil eye.

"Someone besides his uncle has to care," Sister Joan said curtly.

"They'll be looking later." The old woman jerked her shawled head towards the others.

"Why not now?" Sister Joan demanded. "He might have had an accident on the moors, be lying with a broken leg or something on the wet grass."

"There's men already out checking. The rest have their work to do," old Hagar said. "It ain't no use anyways. There's evil here—I've felt it since the night afore last when you and the other one came—no, I'm not saying it came with you so don't bridle up at me. It was here already, creeping and crawling."

"Do you mean someone was here? A prowler?" She spoke sharply.

"Evil," said the old woman provokingly, "looking for something to feed on. Go and pray about that."

"You leave Sister Joan alone, you hear?" Conrad came

loping up, his fists clenched. "You don't want to take no notice of her, Sister. Half crazy she is ever since her old man died."

"At least I had a man," the old woman said slyly and shuffled away with one last vindictive look at Sister Joan's trimly belted waist at which her rosary hung, its beads cool drops of ebony wood, its crucifix of polished copper. Every Daughter of Compassion had an exactly similar rosary presented when she made her final profession. The old woman's taunt had said clearly, "Other females carry babes on their hips. You have a string of beads and a little instrument of torture that you twist into something holy."

Instinctively Sister Joan crossed herself and saw Conrad staring at her.

"She don't really mean any harm," he said, correctly divining her agitation with unchildlike shrewdness. "She's a crazy old bat always going on about doom and death and evil. She doesn't like house dwellers. Come to that she doesn't like travelling people much either."

He laughed, inviting her to lighten the moment with him. She managed a wry smile and went to where Lilith was placidly cropping the grass.

"If Petroc comes back will you ask someone to come up to the convent to let me know?" she asked. "If he isn't back soon then the police will have to be told. You can't not report a missing child."

"We don't like the police here," Conrad said, becoming suddenly all Romany, big hands clenching.

"It isn't always possible to have what we like," Sister Joan said, suddenly impatient with the narrow secretiveness of them all. "You stay here and send me word as soon as Petroc gets back. And go on helping your mother until your father gets home."

"That'll be for ever then," Conrad said, "for he isn't coming back—not ever."

There was no point in arguing especially since she suspected that he was right. From now on Conrad would have to grow fast into manhood, burdened with a precociously sexual sister and a mother who couldn't cope.

Remounting, pulling down the skirt of her habit as one of the men loading scrap turned to give her a long, insolent look, she raised her hand to wave what she trusted looked like a cheerful goodbye to Conrad and rode away from the camp. Rode towards the circle of willows that fringed the pool beyond the noisy wagons and the smell of cooking and urine and damp clothes all mixed up together. It was quite illogical since obviously the first place anyone would have thought of looking was the pool but she rode there anyway.

At twilight it had been an enchanted place, a fragment of Eden with the boy and girl beautiful in their awakening sexuality. Mid morning it was a dark pool, smaller than she had believed, surrounded by the wicker cages of the willows and the dark foliage of the evergreens. There was nothing here, nobody except herself. But when she had stood here with Sister Margaret there might have been another watcher, someone who also had hidden in the blackness of the shadows and watched avidly as the young bodies turned and twisted beneath the surface of the water.

There was no proof of anything at all. Sister Joan chided herself for having an over-active imagination and turned Lilith homeward. For the moment there was nothing more she could do.

"You're home very early, Sister." Mother Dorothy looked up from the letter she was reading as Sister Joan tapped on the parlour door and entered.

The parlour had been a double drawing-room in the days when the Tarquins owned the house. It retained its polished floor, its gilded cornices, even the panels of embroidered silk on the walls, but the great mirrored cabinets, the huge sofas and velvet seated wing chairs had gone. A functional desk and straight backed chairs now furnished the huge, chilly room and no Aubusson carpets softened her footsteps on the polished floor.

"I decided to close school early, Mother," Sister Joan said, briefly kneeling for the customary blessing. "The Romany children hadn't turned up and then Mr. Lee came by to tell me that Petroc had been missing since last night. He offered to take the other children home and I rode over to the camp to see if I could make any sense out of it all. I'm afraid I went there without permission, but I thought it important to begin enquiries as quickly as possible."

"And you would naturally want first-hand information." Mother Dorothy spoke with a certain dryness. "I believe your action was quite justified in the circumstances. What did you find out?"

"That nobody's laid eyes on Petroc since he went out last evening. He didn't take any money with him, and he obviously didn't return—not even at midnight when it started to rain."

"But surely a child would be expected home before midnight?" the prioress said.

"Romany children grow up fast, Mother, and Petroc's parents aren't with him. His mother ran off and his father's in gaol for receiving stolen goods," Sister Joan explained. "His uncle, Padraic Lee is doing his best but he has two daughters of his own and his wife—she has a drink problem. Petroc's twelve and very self-reliant, so his going missing wouldn't cause an immediate outcry."

"But the police are now handling it, I assume?"

"Not yet, Mother. Mr. Lee went into Bodmin after he'd taken the other children home, so he might find out something there, and some of the other men in the camp went to search the moors, but they distrust the authorities. However if Petroc doesn't turn up within the next couple of hours I've insisted that his disappearance be reported."

"Quite right, Sister. What feckless beings they must be," Mother Dorothy said, hunching her shoulders in disapproval.

"I asked Conrad—he's another of my pupils—to make sure that someone sends word here as soon as Petroc is found. I hope that was all right?"

"Very sensible, Sister. You obviously cannot go running round looking for him yourself but you are bound to feel a certain responsibility in the matter. I will tell Sister Margaret to expect a telephone call and I will go myself to the chapel after the midday meal to pray that all is well. You might consider having a word with the local social worker at some future date if conditions at the camp continue to be unsatisfactory. So you have the afternoon free which is most fortunate."

"Yes, Mother?" Sister Joan looked dutifully expectant.

"Sister Hilaria has lost a filling out of her tooth which is causing her considerable discomfort and may lead to more problems with her other teeth. I rang up the dentist in Bodmin and he very obligingly agreed to fit her in at 2:30 this afternoon. I intended to ask Sister Margaret to drive her in but Sister Margaret already went over to the presbytery this morning to get more holy water from Father Malone, so I hesitate to send her off again. You drive, don't you, Sister Joan?"

"Mother Dorothy, I haven't driven for years—not since I entered the religious life," Sister Joan said in alarm.

"Did you keep your licence up to date?"

"Yes, Mother, but only because Mother Agnes was of the opinion that I'd be foolish to let it lapse when in the future I might need to drive somewhere."

"That was most far-sighted of Mother Agnes," Mother Dorothy approved. "You see, the necessity has arisen. You may take Sister Hilaria to the dentist and, at the same time, buy yourself a pair of neat trousers to wear under your habit when you ride the horse. It appears that shop-bought trousers are superior to anything that can be run up here. I understand that the cost will be in the region of thirty pounds which does seem very high, so if you can manage to bring me some change I'll be very grateful. However don't get inferior workmanship; that's a false economy."

"No, Mother. Thank you, Mother." Accepting the money Sister Joan felt bound to add, "But as to driving—I am dreadfully out of practice."

"I imagine it is rather like swimming or bike riding," her superior said briskly. "Once learnt the accomplishment is never forgotten. You understand that this is a privilege, Sister? Sister Margaret will continue to drive on all ordinary occasions."

"Yes, Mother." Sister Joan genuflected respectfully and somehow or other got herself out of the parlour.

Sister Hilaria whose expression as she ate the midday meal proved that she was trying to conceal the fact that she was in considerable pain, waited for her afterwards, looking with her vaguely distracted air rather like a large, absent-minded child about to be taken out for a treat. She had the slightly prominent eyes of the mystic and big clumsy hands at variance with a delicate Modigliani face. Her voice, breathless and husky, had a singsong quality. It was as if she were so unsuited to everyday living that her mystic experiences, of which she seldom spoke, had been given to her as a special grace to compensate for her inadequacies in every other direction. Sister Joan, having thought that, immediately reminded herself that Mother Dorothy had retained Sister Hilaria as novice mistress and that the other must have capabilities not visible to general view.

"It is very good of you to relieve Sister Margaret and take me into town," she said as they went round to the back. "I would not have complained but Mother Dorothy noticed the swelling in my cheek, so under obedience I was constrained to tell."

"You should have told anyway, Sister. There's no merit in hiding pain," Sister Joan said, adopting the faintly scolding tone that everybody unconsciously picked up when talking to Sister Hilaria.

"It seemed so unimportant," Sister Hilaria said vaguely, "but it will be a relief to have it fixed. Isn't it sad to think how dependent we are on our bodies?"

"Since we're in them we might as well treat them properly," Sister Joan argued. "Oh, Sister Margaret, may I please have the car keys? Did Mother Dorothy tell you—?"

"Just before dinner, Sister. I gave the seats a bit of a polish," Sister Margaret said cheerfully, handing over the keys. "Now don't worry about your driving. Just trust in Our Dear Lord and you'll come safe home. Sister Hilaria, if you get a draught in that tooth you'll know about it. Put your scarf around your mouth."

"You don't think the effect might be a little—gangster-ish?" Sister Hilaria asked anxiously as she complied.

"Don't worry, Sister," Sister Joan advised as they climbed into the car. "When people see the standard of my driving I'm the one who'll be mistaken for a gangster. Fasten your seatbelt."

She turned the ignition and let in the clutch gingerly, wishing as she eased the vehicle out of the yard that Sister Margaret hadn't crossed herself and said, "God and the blessed saints bring you safely back," with quite so much fervour.

Yet within a few minutes she had settled comfortably enough into the rhythm of driving again, skirting the gate-posts without mishap and taking the moor road that led across the greenway towards the huddled roofs of Bodmin. Neither could she stop herself from glancing around as she drove, hoping to see a dishevelled young boy waving at her. Nothing human met her roving gaze. Only sheep, their lambs close to their sides, cropped the turf. It was always possible that Petroc was already safely back at the camp, but her instincts doubted it.

They had reached the greenway with the chimneys of the old Druid place crowding the skyline. Slowing down she found herself wondering why the Olives had chosen to settle in such a remote house. Perhaps Clive Olive intended to farm the land but there was no sign of any activity that would have suggested planting or sowing; perhaps they were very rich and wanted to live a quiet rural life, but they had done very little to renovate or furnish the little she had seen of the interior. Neither had there been any evidence of domestic staff apart from the beautiful young man.

As if thought had conjured him he emerged from the front gate, causing her to brake sharply.

"Sister Joan! Sister Joan!" Samantha ran out behind the young man, waving her arm. Sister Joan stopped and wound down her window.

"Good afternoon, Samantha. You got home safely then?"

"Mr. Lee took everybody," Samantha said. "He's a very agreeable man for a gypsy."

"Indeed he is." Sister Joan nodded, reminding herself that a lesson on the evils of racial discrimination might not come amiss in the near future. "Is this the new au pair?"

She nodded towards the young man who had paused and was regarding them gravely.

"Jan Heinz," Samantha said. "Just like the baked beans. He's part Dutch and part German and altogether rather backward. He speaks hardly any English at all."

"That certainly doesn't mean he's backward," Sister Joan reproved. "You will have to help him learn the language. You helped Kiki—what was her name?"

"Kiki Svenson. She spoke English in a funny kind of way. She was nice," Samantha said wistfully.

"You said she left suddenly." Sister Joan tried to sound casual.

"In the middle of the night," Samantha said.

"But how could you know that? You'd have been asleep and in bed," Sister Joan said.

"I was," Samantha said, "but when I got up in the morning Kiki wasn't around. My mum said she'd upped and gone in the middle of the night. She'd taken all her things and just vanished. I daresay she didn't much like having to do housework."

"When was this?"

"About three weeks ago. Why?"

"This is such a beautiful part of the country," Sister Joan said vaguely. "Well, I have to get Sister Hilaria to the dentist. Try and talk to Jan. He will soon pick up English, I'm sure."

She sent a brisk encouraging smile towards the young man who smiled back uncertainly.

"Are we coming to school tomorrow, Sister?" Samantha asked. "We don't have to stay away because Petroc's missing?"

"Oh, I'm sure he'll be back tomorrow," Sister Joan said encouragingly. "Certainly there'll be school for everybody."

"I hope he comes back," Samantha said as Sister Joan started up the car again. "He is a nice person, I think. Handsome."

"Very handsome." Sister Joan felt a twinge of amused sympathy as she drove off. Samantha was growing up, beginning to notice the opposite sex, to fix her affections on first one and then another, rehearsing for the real love that would doubtless grip her one day. That it was highly unlikely Petroc would ever regard the plain little Olive girl in any romantic light gave a poignancy to her childish feelings.

"I'm sorry for the delay, Sister." She flashed an apologetic glance at her silent companion. "Samantha Olive is one of my pupils and as we are all worried about Petroc I felt obliged to stop for a moment."

"I was looking at the young man," Sister Hilaria said, lowering her scarf slightly to reveal a swollen cheek. "I was recalling that Lucifer was the most beautiful of the angels."

"Hardly Lucifer, Sister, merely a young foreigner hoping to learn the language. It is quite fashionable these days to employ a male au pair or nanny, I believe."

"Modern life is very bewildering," Sister Hilaria said. "You would be astonished at some of the things my two postulants tell me. Ah, we are coming into Bodmin now, aren't we? The last time I was here was six years ago when I had my tooth filled, so it is quite a treat to see it again."

"If I leave you at the dentist's and go to buy the trousers," Sister Joan said, "you won't mind waiting?"

"Not at all, Sister. I recall I had an injection last time that froze my face and made the subsequent treatment completely painless," Sister Hilaria assured her.

Sister Joan slowed to a crawl and negotiated herself and her passenger through the Thursday afternoon traffic with a trepidation that was scarcely justified. It was astonishing how quickly one became used to being behind the wheel again.

The dentist's was easily located. Sister Hilaria, assured that she would be called for in half an hour, alighted from the car and went in. Sister Joan drove on into the parking lot and congratulated herself on getting into a free space with the minimum of difficulty.

There was a new supermarket at the end of the street, wire baskets fitted together at the entrance with a notice informing intending customers that a deposit of a pound was required. The deposit would be returned, but Sister Joan, looking in some bewilderment at the large slot machine with its pulleys, decided she could buy a pair of pants without a basket, and bravely marched into the air-conditioned, neon-lit interior.

In every direction stretched long aisles lined with shelves containing every possible variety of merchandise. It was an Arabian Nights' cave of temptation and wonder, she thought, and felt a sense of unreality. It was six years since she'd entered a shop of any kind and, for a moment, she felt completely disoriented. Then she saw the ranks of skirts and jeans and slacks and headed for them like a Bedouin making for his local oasis.

"Need any help, Sister?" A salesgirl with a pert, pretty face was hovering.

"I am supposed to buy a pair of hard wearing trousers for riding," Sister Joan said, "but I'm spoilt for choice."

"We don't do jodhpurs, Sister," the girl began.

"A decent pair of jeans will do very well, in my size. I ride a horse to the school where I teach," Sister Joan said, feeling that some explanation was required.

"You'll be from the convent up on the moors. I didn't think they ever let any of you out," the girl said artlessly.

"Oh, I got remission for good behaviour," Sister Joan said mischievously. "I'm waist twenty-five inches, hips thirty-six."

"It's all centimeters now," the girl said. "Look, these seem about right. Take this pair along to the changing-room and see if they'll do. If they're OK then you just take them to the check-out and the assistant there removes the magnetic tag. Easy."

"Thank you very much. You've been very helpful." With the jeans over her arm she turned in the direction of the changing-rooms, and went into one of the cubicles.

There was a full-length mirror against one wall. For an instant she felt an actual, physical shock at the sight of her own full-length reflection. During the past six years she had lived without looking glasses in a world where neatness and cleanliness were all that was necessary. Personal vanity had—was supposed to have no place. Part glimpses of her reflection in the darkened glass of a door, the surface of a copper dish, a fragment of her features in the little mirror in Petroc's wagon, hardly registered at the time, were the total of her knowledge of her contemporary being.

The woman in the long mirror looked younger than her mid-thirties as if time had stood still since she had entered the religious life. Her figure had remained trim, fortunately since she was below the average height; her skin was tight and rosy with a scattering of freckles across the snub nose; long lashed blue eyes looked out at the world from the frame of white wimple and veil. When she smiled at herself her nose crinkled slightly. Jacob had often teased her about that.

You're a nice looking woman, she told her reflection silently. The religious life suits you.

There was no vanity in the realization, merely the acknowledgement of a fact. She bent in the cramped space to remove her shoes and pull on the jeans, relieved to find that they fitted well. Taking them off again, refastening her shoes, she left the cubicle and was paying for her purchase at the check-out before it dawned on her that she hadn't even bothered to look in the mirror again.

The rain had ceased and the sun was gilding the street when she emerged from the supermarket. Around her shoppers eddied and swirled. There was still plenty of time before she had to meet Sister Hilaria. She contemplated a spot of window shopping and rejected it. Window shopping was definitely time wasting. Much more sensible to put her parcel in the back of the car and then go and wait for her companion.

She was relocking the boot of the car, straightening up when a gleam of sunlight dazzled her momentarily. Putting up her hand to shield her eyes, turning slightly from the glare, she read clearly across the road at the other side of the parking space, FOREIGN HELP, the au pair agency from where the Olives had hired Kiki Svenson and now Jan Heinz. That she should notice it now seemed like a clear signal. Putting the car keys into her purse along with the five pounds change for Mother Dorothy she walked briskly across to the agency with its pleasant reception area, brightened with pot plants and with easy chairs contrasting with businesslike filing cabinets and a desk at which a grey-haired woman sat.

"Good afternoon, Sister. May I help you?" The voice was amiable as was the smile. If the woman wondered what a nun was doing in an agency that specialized in the hiring of foreign domestic help she didn't allow it to show.

"Good afternoon. I'm Sister Joan from the Daughters of Compassion—oh, no, I'm not collecting for anything." She flushed as the woman reached for her handbag with a resigned air. "I came to make enquiries about a girl— an au pair."

"For the convent?" The other allowed her surprise to peep out.

"No, not exactly. A girl called Kiki Svenson—she worked for the Olives—?"

"She came very highly recommended," the other said. "I was surprised to hear from Mrs. Olive that she'd left. If she had been dissatisfied she could have come to us and we would have tried to relocate her."

"She didn't come to you?"

"She stayed barely a month and then took off. Mrs. Olive was most put out about it. However we were able to fix her up with a young man just on our books who wishes to spend a year learning to speak English. I do hope—?"

"Jan Heinz is proving most satisfactory, I understand," Sister Joan said. "I did wonder if you had Kiki Svenson's home address. I'd like to get in touch with her—it's a private matter, you understand. I hardly like to ask Mrs. Olive."

"Miss Svenson didn't mention she was a Catholic." The woman turned to extract a file from one of the cabinets. "Ah, she gave two addresses. Her home address which Mrs. Olive will also have and a London address. I believe she mentioned having done some hotel work in London before deciding she would like to sample rural living. I can give you both, Sister.''

"That's very kind of you," Sister Joan said, watching the other copy the two addresses. "You didn't contact her yourself after she left?''

"We had no reason to do so. The girl was of full age and quite competent. Sister, there isn't anything wrong, is there?''

"I hope not," Sister Joan said as she put the slip of paper in her purse. "I do hope not. Thank you.''

Hurrying out, she was aware of the woman's concerned gaze following her.

SEVEN

✠ ✠ ✠

Sister Hilaria, looking somewhat paler than even her usual delicate colour, was in the waiting-room, scarf to her face, when Sister Joan arrived.

"The tooth," she said indistinctly, "had to come out. Fortunately it's a side one and won't affect my chewing. The dentist said I ought to have a warm drink, so I wonder if we might have one in a local cafe before we drive back?"

"And a couple of aspirins," Sister Joan said, her own jaw beginning to ache in sympathy. "There's a nice cafe just down the street, Sister, and a chemist's right next door."

"I have some pocket money." Sister Hilaria looked around as if she expected it to drop out of the sky.

"My treat. I have some pocket money too."

The change for Mother Dorothy would go back untouched. Of the five pounds a month given to every sister out of which she could buy small necessities, postage stamps and the like, Sister Joan still had four pounds and sixty pence. Wondering vaguely what she had squandered forty pence on she shepherded Sister Hilaria to the cafe, seated her at a corner table, ordered two coffees, nipped into the chemist to purchase aspirin, and returned, slightly breathless, with the pleasant conviction that living in a convent hadn't impaired her ability to function in the ordinary world.

"This is quite a little indulgence," Sister Hilaria said happily, fanning her coffee cup with a paper napkin. "Really, I feel quite dissipated, Sister. In the nicest possible way, of course. It is almost worth having a tooth out."

Between her and Sister Margaret there was a great similarity, Sister Joan thought as she sipped her own coffee. Both had the gift of serenity. Nothing marred their private space. She wondered if she would ever achieve the same untroubled purity of spirit.

"Isn't that the gentleman who brings fish to the convent?" Sister Hilaria asked, glancing through the window.

"It's Padraic Lee, yes." Sister Joan half rose but he had spotted them and was entering the cafe.

"Sister Joan, I thought as how it was you. Sister." Seeing her companion he touched his forelock in an old-fashioned gesture that should have looked ridiculous but didn't.

"Sister Hilaria is the novice mistress," Sister Joan said. "She has just had a tooth out."

"Nasty." He clicked his tongue in sympathy. "Sister Joan, I'm glad I ran into you. I've been everywhere I can think of to ask but there's no sign of Petroc. I went back to the camp but nobody's seen a sign of him. Young Hagar said they took a walk up by the pool last evening but it looked like rain so she came back. She'd had a row with her brother, Conrad, on account of him telling her she didn't help out sufficient, so she went off in a paddy and met Petroc up by the willows."

"And?—please, sit down. I'll get you a cup of coffee," Sister Joan said.

"Nothing for me, thank you. I've a fancy for something stronger to tell you the truth and that's not like me." He pulled up a spare chair and sat down, his brow furrowed. "I questioned Hagar close and she said she'd let off steam a bit about Conrad and Petroc said he saw her point of view and then he said he had to go and ran off and she came back to camp."

"He didn't say where he was going?"

"Not according to Hagar. She called after him that it looked like rain and he called back that he'd soon be under cover. That's all. Sister, I fear we'll have to report he's missing, little though I enjoy meddling with the law."

"That's a very sensible decision," Sister Joan approved.

"In fact I was on my way to the station when I saw you through the window," Padraic continued. "I was wondering if you might—possibly—?" He hesitated.

"You would like Sister Joan to report it," Sister Hilaria said surprisingly.

"That's the way of it. Truth is that I'm never—comfortable in a police station," he said. "Mind, I've no criminal record but I never did trust a uniform."

"I'm sure Sister Joan would be happy to help out," Sister Hilaria said. "If you can wait while I take another aspirin—"

"Sister Hilaria, you ought to be back at the convent resting, not running around Bodmin," Sister Joan said, observing the other's increasing pallor with alarm.

"I fear you are correct, Sister. The injection has certainly made me feel not quite myself," Sister Hilaria admitted. "Mr. Lee, if you would be so kind as to take me back in your vehicle then Sister Joan can follow in the car when she has made her report to the police officers. I will explain the circumstances to Mother Dorothy.''

''It's only a lorry,'' Padraic said doubtfully.

''Splendid. Sister Joan, thank you for the coffee. Most refreshing. Mr. Lee?'' She rose, pulling the scarf up to her swollen cheek, and preceded Padraic to the door.

''You'll make it clear, Sister,'' he lingered to say, ''that the kids are well looked after? I'd not want them social workers messing round.''

''I'll do my best,'' she promised, and watched him hurry after Sister Hilaria.

The police station was at the corner of the next road, a panda car drawn up outside, the young policeman behind the wheel giving her an incurious glance as she went up the steps. Or had he been as young as all that? Perhaps she was ageing more rapidly than she had fancied.

''May I help you, Sister?'' The policeman behind the desk was certainly verging on middle age. Sister Joan drew a breath and launched forth.

''I am Sister Joan from the Order of the Daughters of Compassion. I also teach at the school up on the moor.''

''Yes?'' A faint spark of interest had come into his heavy face. Probably he recalled the events of the previous year that had ended so tragically for some.*

''One of my pupils has been missing since last evening. His uncle has asked me to report the matter.''

''Why not come in himself?''

''The child is from the Romany camp.''

''A gyppo, eh?''

''A Romany child,'' she corrected, wincing slightly. ''I said that I would come in and give you the details.''

''Right then. Oh, come round and sit down, Sister.''

*See ''Vow of Silence''

He lifted the wooden barrier, indicated a chair, and drew a form toward him.

"The child's name is Petroc Lee," Sister Joan said. "He's twelve years old, tall for his age, slim with dark eyes and hair, olive skin, gold ring in one ear. I don't know what he was wearing—jeans and sweater, I imagine."

"Would his uncle be Padraic Lee?" The policeman looked up.

"Yes. The boy's father is in gaol—a minor offence, I believe, and his mother left. Do you know Mr. Lee?"

"I do and a right—pleasant gentleman he seems to be," the policeman said, meeting her steady gaze and obviously amending what he had intended to say.

"Mr. Lee shows a great interest in the welfare of his nephew," Sister Joan said. "He tells me that he saw the child last evening going off somewhere and assumed when the rain began at midnight that he'd already returned to his own wagon. This morning the wagon was empty with no signs of anyone having slept in it. I went up to the camp myself and, with permission, looked round the wagon myself. Nothing seems to have been taken and he left his money box behind."

"And you sorted through everything and left your prints everywhere, Sister?"

"Prints? Why, yes, I suppose I did but I didn't think—"

"The public," he said sadly, "never does. Go on. Was his uncle the last person to see him?"

"His friend, Hagar Smith, another of my pupils, walked with him as far as the trees fringing the pool. He said he had somewhere to go and ran off."

"Anything else?" His biro was poised.

"Apparently—I have this only at second hand from Mr.

Lee—Petroc said he'd soon be under cover, referring to the threatened rain which didn't actually begin until later.''

"How old is this Hagar?" He was making notes.

"Hagar Smith. She's twelve. Her brother, Conrad, is also in my school." Realizing that she was beginning to chatter nervously she bit her lip.

"It's not our concern if they haven't moved on into the secondary school," he said. "If the education authority's content they're getting an adequate education then it's fine by us. Would you say this Hagar is a truthful child?"

"She's never told me a lie to my knowledge."

"And the boy? Ever been in trouble?"

"Not as far as I know. He's lively."

"I don't suppose you have a photograph?"

She shook her head regretfully. "The Romanies are apt to be superstitious about having their photographs taken. His uncle may have one somewhere."

"Left it a bit late to report a missing child, haven't you?" He was reaching for the telephone.

"I only learned of it this morning when Mr. Lee came over to the school to see if Petroc had turned up there. I gave the children the rest of the day off and went first to the camp—leaving my fingerprints." She made an apologetic little gesture. "I had to come into town with one of the other sisters who required dental treatment, and we met Mr. Lee again. He told me there had been a search but without results and asked me to come here."

"Can you let me have a list of your pupils?" He turned away, talking rapidly into the telephone, giving details of the paper he had just filled in.

"Why?" Sister Joan asked when he turned to her again. "Why do you need the other names? I'm sure they don't know anything helpful."

"As to that we'll have to see, won't we, Sister? If the

lad was going somewhere last evening maybe he mentioned something to one of the others. You've only got a small school, haven't you?''

"Ten pupils when they're all there.''

"Yes?'' He had taken another piece of paper and was looking at her expectantly.

"Mr. Lee's two little girls, Tabitha and Edith, attend. They're aged six and seven, and they're cousins to Petroc. Then there's Petroc himself, and the two Smith children, Conrad and Hagar. The other Romany children are either too young for school or attend the one in Bodmin—when they attend anywhere.''

"And the other five?''

"The Penglow children, Madelyn and David come to the school. They'll both start in Bodmin next term; Timothy Holt, the son of a local farmer—the Penglows are farmers too—Billy Wesley, a bit of a harum scarum but a nice boy, and Samantha Olive—they are newcomers to the district. Samantha is eleven.''

"Would you be kind enough to jot down their addresses, Sister?'' He passed paper and pen to her, rose and went into an inner room. There was the murmur of voices.

She wrote steadily, finishing just as he returned.

"All done, Sister? That'll be very useful.''

"I've added the telephone numbers where there are any,'' she pointed out. "Sergeant, I don't want you to think that because Petroc is a Romany child his relatives are not concerned about him. The children from the camp grow up fast, become self-reliant at an early age, but their families still care.''

"So,'' said the sergeant, "do the police. One more thing, Sister. Could you step into the back and permit us to take your fingerprints for elimination purposes?''

"Yes, of course. I'm afraid that I simply didn't think—you're going to search the wagon? That doesn't mean—?"

"It means we're making routine enquiries. Sister. Don't start imagining what isn't there," he advised.

She bit back a retort and followed him meekly. A couple of officers were studying a map of the district, glancing up briefly as she went in.

"Just dip your fingers in this, Sister. You can wash your hands immediately you've finished. Officer Lloyd will see to you."

Obediently she submitted, washed her hands at the small sink in the corner, and stood uncertainly until the desk sergeant came over again.

"As soon as the lad turns up your prints will be destroyed," he said. "No need to worry on that score."

"I wasn't," she said with dignity.

"Now will you want transport home?" He looked at her with a kindly air. "You said you were with another nun?"

"She got a lift from Mr. Lee and I have the convent car here."

"The one Sister Margaret drives?" He raised his eyes briefly to heaven. "All right, Sister. Thank you for coming in. Try not to worry."

As well tell the wind not to blow, she reflected, coming out into the street. Petroc had been missing now for nearly twenty-four hours.

There remained one other task for her to do before she drove back to the convent. She had contemplated mentioning it to the sergeant but his remark about imagining things had effectively silenced her. The trouble was that she might be imagining that something needed to be explained about Kiki Svenson's abrupt departure from the Olive household.

She walked to the nearest call box, took the slip of paper out of her purse, and dialled the London number. Later on she would think about the fact that she was making a telephone call without permission.

"Yes?" The voice at the other end was female, middle-aged, slightly husky.

"May I speak to Kiki Svenson, please?"

"If I knew where she was you could," the voice said wearily. "I've had a procession of boyfriends on the telephone, not to mention her family. Not one word in over a month—and no rent paid."

"You knew she went down to Cornwall?"

"As an au pair? Yes, she mentioned it, asked me to hold her room in case she didn't like it. Paid a month in advance before she left—and then nothing. It's not good enough. I don't rent out bedsitters for fun."

"I'm sure you don't." Sister Joan spoke rapidly, afraid the other might hang up. "My name is Sister Joan; I'm a nun at the local convent here. If I give you the convent telephone number would you give it to Miss Svenson when she returns and ask her to ring me immediately. It's important."

"I'll get a pencil," the voice at the other end said wearily.

Sister Joan gave the number clearly, repeated her name, assured the landlady that she was sure Kiki would be back soon with an explanation and the missing rent and hung up, the feeling of sickness inside her intensifying. Not a physical sickness but a reaction of her body to mental strain, she thought clinically, and drew several long, satisfying breaths as she came out of the close confines of the kiosk.

The afternoon was well advanced. She would have to hurry or miss the cup of tea the sisters drank before they retired to their cells or to the library for the two hours of religious studies that preceded Benediction.

"What makes you think that you'll be able to stand the routine?" Jacob had mocked when she had made it clear her decision was firm. "You find it hard to wake up in time for your Sunday mass."

"It will be very good for me," she had retorted then. "I need something to keep me in order."

"What's so good about order? What's wrong with a little divine untidiness?" he had demanded.

Jacob had been wrong, she thought, walking rapidly to the car. There had to be order to provide the loom on which one could weave a life. Whatever the outer and inner troubles that preoccupied her there was always the unchanging routine of the convent day to remind her that stability was the framework of existence.

"We are not an entirely closed Order," her former prioress had said. "The founder of the Daughters of Compassion believed that it was possible to combine Saint Martha and Saint Mary Magdalene in a well-rounded life. To earn a living is a praiseworthy occupation, whether as teacher, librarian, nurse—anything that serves the community at large in a lawful way. But the work must rest upon a solid foundation of prayer, worship, contemplation."

Sister Joan wondered what Jacob would say if he were to meet her now, to hear that after six years she would have felt lost without the two hours of devotions that began every day, the two hours of religious study that brought the working day to a close and the evenings filled by Benediction, a meatless supper, an hour of recreation during which each sister must have her hands occupied with sewing or knitting, the final half-hour in chapel, the blessing that marked the start of the grand silence. By 9:30 she was in bed when six or seven years before she would have been putting on her eye-shadow and sallying forth to a wine bar. The woman of six years before would, she thought, have read in the newspaper about the disappearance of a child, said indignantly that there were some wicked people in the world, and turned the page.

She drove back at a moderate speed, becoming increasingly confident as her old skill revived, but unwilling to relinquish the sense of mobility and freedom that being behind the wheel brought. It was also, she thought ruefully, a way of postponing the inevitable when alone with her thoughts she would have to decide how far she was entitled to involve herself in Kiki Svenson's disappearance, in the search for Petroc Lee.

Sister Margaret was hovering anxiously in the yard when she drove up, her round face relaxing into a smile as Sister Joan alighted.

"No problems with the car, Sister?"

"Not even a scrape," Sister Joan assured her, handing over the keys.

"Our Dear Lord would certainly not have allowed anything to happen while you were on a mission of mercy," Sister Margaret said comfortably. "Sister Hilaria has gone to lie down until suppertime. Fortunately it's soup tonight, so she won't need to chew much. Did you report the little boy's disappearance to the police? We have all been praying about it."

"The police were very kind. They've started their enquiries."

"Then we must hope for a happy result, mustn't we? Oh, Mother Dorothy would like to have a word."

"Thank you, Sister."

Tapping on the parlour door she reminded herself that she had a telephone call on her conscience.

"Sister Hilaria arrived home in a lorry," the prioress said without preamble. "I doubt if it gives a very good impression to the neighbourhood when Daughters of Compassion are seen whizzing around in lorries with somewhat suspect companions. However for this one occasion it has to be tolerated. It was most sensible of you to take Sister for a warm drink. The tooth extraction was more painful than she will admit. You have seen the police?"

"Yes, Mother Dorothy. They took down all the details."

"We will pray that there is a happy result. Boys do sometimes wander off and think it a great adventure," Mother Dorothy said. "But these days—the world sometimes seems to me to be regressing into barbarism. Is something else on your mind, Sister Joan?"

"Yes, Reverend Mother," Sister Joan said simply.

"Yet you hesitate to confide in me. No, don't jerk your chin at me in that undutiful manner. It is a most eloquent chin but it cannot alter facts. I am well aware that since you came to us last year you have found it difficult to accept me as prioress instead of your former prioress in your mother house. Mother Agnes is a woman of subtle and godly gifts, Sister. If the rest of us find it difficult to live up to her high standards then you must bear with us."

"Mother Dorothy, I never meant to imply—" Sister Joan began, horrified.

"I was elected as prioress because, I suspect, the community felt that a practical person was required here. This entire convent was tipping over into hysterical nonsense. You helped to bring it to an end for which we owe you gratitude, but it must be sometimes a temptation to wish for more excitement, a cause, a white horse to ride. You do not talk over problems with your superior because you like her personally. You do so as a matter of obedience.''

"I took action without asking first for permission,'' Sister Joan said.

"There is an American term, I believe,'' Mother Dorothy said. "So tell me something new—that is how it goes. What is your latest misdemeanour, Sister Joan?''

"When I'd made the report to the police I made a telephone call. I ought to have returned first to the convent and asked for permission, but I didn't.''

"Whom did you telephone?''

"This number. I think it's a lodging house—in London. The Olives' au pair was staying there before she came into Cornwall. She left the Olives' employment suddenly—their little girl, Samantha, told me she disappeared in the middle of the night. I wanted to be sure she was all right—in view of Petroc's also being missing.''

"Where did you obtain the telephone number?''

"From the Agency in town, while Sister Hilaria was in the dentist's. The woman in the office gave me Kiki Svenson's home address in Sweden and her London lodging.''

"You certainly didn't sit idle while Sister Hilaria was being treated, did you?'' Mother Dorothy said dryly. "What was the result of your enquiry?''

"The landlady said that Kiki Svenson left a couple of months ago, saying she'd be back if she didn't like it in Cornwall. She paid an extra month's rent and left a few of her things there. Since then she hasn't heard a word.''

"And the Olives' child told you that the girl had left in the middle of the night?''

"I suppose either Mr. or Mrs. Olive could have driven her to the station,'' Sister Joan said, "but there aren't any trains in the middle of the night. Even if there'd been a quarrel of some kind she'd surely have waited until morning.''

"To a child, nine in the evening can seem like the middle of the night.''

"Samantha is eleven and very bright, Mother. She didn't see the girl leave. She told me that she disappeared 'just like Petroc Lee' she said.''

"Because she makes a completely unsubstantial connection between the two events is no reason for us to fall into the same error,'' Mother Dorothy said. "However, it does appear to me that the girl seems to have left rather abruptly and her not going to pick up her things is worrying. Did you say anything to the police?''

"No, Mother Dorothy.''

"Very wise of you. There is no point in starting rumours when there will probably be a perfectly simple explanation. I shall write express to Miss Svenson's home address, asking her to contact me if she is at home. No, Sister, there is no use in glancing hopefully towards the telephone. Ringing up Sweden is not allowed for in the community budget. An express letter will serve the purpose. Did you leave a message at the lodging house?''

"I asked that she ring the convent as soon as she returned, Mother.''

"Then you seem to have done everything necessary, Sister. You behaved impetuously, but I would not like you to think that obedience completely precludes any independence of thought or action. You visited the Olives with Sister Margaret, did you not? What were your impressions?''

"They've taken the old Druid place, Mother. Julia Olive is very elegant, about my age, rather languid in manner. Her husband, Clive Olive, came in briefly. He is older than her, has a built up shoe—possibly a club foot.

He is writing a book, he said. They were both very pleasant, obviously good parents. Samantha is always nicely
dressed and punctual. The au pair brings her to school
and picks her up.''

"Who brings her now?''

"The new au pair. It—he is a young man, part Dutch,
part German. Very beautiful.''

"Beautiful, Sister Joan?''

"Sister Hilaria saw him when we went by on our way
to the dentist. She remarked that he looked like Lucifer.''

"One trusts that dear Sister Hilaria was speaking met-
aphorically,'' Mother Dorothy observed, her eyebrows
shooting up. "I would not like to think that any of our
Order had a first hand knowledge of that gentleman. You
didn't mention the former au pair to anyone else?''

"No, Reverend Mother.''

"You obtained the—er trousers for riding?''

"Oh, yes, Mother. And there's five pounds change,''
Sister Joan remembered, delving into her purse.

"Thank you, Sister. Now I suggest that you try to put
all of this out of your mind and go to your religious studies. What line are you pursuing at the moment?''

"The history of the rosary devotion, Mother.''

"Meditate upon the rule, child. Poverty, chastity, obedience and compassion—the four branches of our Order.
They must be held in balance. Think about them. Think
about them positively—and Sister, at general confession
you need not mention the telephone call. Your last confession was quite sufficiently startling. Our two postulants
sat there with the most peculiar expressions on their
faces.''

"Yes, Reverend Mother.'' Kneeling for the brisk blessing, she was emboldened to add, "May I apologize for
my lack of candour?''

"Which was inadvertent, I'm sure. Thank you, Sister Joan."

Put Petroc Lee and Kiki Svenson out of your mind and concentrate on your religious duties, she instructed herself firmly as she made her way to her cell.

Peace reigned over the convent. Seated cross-legged on the floor, Sister Joan dragged her mind back to the implications of the rule for the community as a whole, for each individual nun.

The bell tinkled for Benediction. Filing into chapel with the others she clung to the illusion of tranquillity. After Benediction, supper, with the promised soup and an omelette. Sister Hilaria looked better after her rest. The reading was from a study of Saint Mary Magdalene. The sinner turned saint, according to tradition. Love wasn't always sexual even between human beings. It could be transcended. Hagar and Petroc swimming in the pool. "A dirty house," Sister Margaret had said. It had been neat and tidy, if over heated. Evil crawling.

She jerked from a momentary doze as Sister Perpetua closed the book with a little bang.

They filed into the big recreation room, clutching their sewing and knitting. Mother Dorothy had joined them, keeping the conversation on a light note, not touching on the disappearance of the child. There was more to her prioress than she had yet appreciated, she decided, and found herself smiling.

"Such an amusing little anecdote," Sister Martha was saying. "It was in the book about the child saints. I wish I could recall it properly."

"Shall I get the book for you from the library, Sister?" Sister Joan offered.

It was not entirely a charitable gesture. Sitting still with a half-finished scarf dangling from the needles was not her notion of a wildly amusing occupation.

"That would be kind, Sister. You know the book I mean." Sister Martha whose feet were hurting smiled her gratitude.

"Reverend Mother, Sisters, please excuse me for one moment." Putting down the despised knitting she hurried out, down the stairs, across the hall into the chapel passage known officially as the cloister though it wasn't one. The light had almost faded and the sanctuary lamp in the chapel glowed like a beacon.

She turned to the altar, genuflected, was frozen into the kneeling pose as if she had been turned to stone.

Petroc lay below the altar on the wide step, arms crossed and eyes closed, a slim young knight who had never ridden into battle. His jeans and sweater were dark in the glow of the sanctuary lamp. For an instant there flared the wild hope that he would jump up and shout, "Boo, Sister Joan! Did I give you a fright?"

He didn't move. Rising unsteadily, moving with slow, reluctant steps towards the altar, she knew even before she touched his hand that he would never move again.

EIGHT

✠ ✠ ✠

"Reverend Mother, may I speak with you privately?"

She had waited a moment or two to compose herself before returning to the recreation room.

Mother Dorothy shot one keen glance at her face and rose at once, her voice brisk and ordinary.

"Sister David, please go on with what you were saying. Excuse me, Sisters." Outside, the door closed, she asked in a lower voice, "What is it, Sister? You look exceedingly pale."

"Petroc Lee is lying below the altar, Mother. He's—he's dead."

The prioress wasted no time on further questioning. She turned and went swiftly down the stairs, Sister Joan at her heels.

The latter had the sudden thought that this incident might be like the brief disappearance of the crucifix again. Perhaps Petroc wouldn't be there when they entered the chapel.

Petroc was still there, lying in exactly the same position. Mother Dorothy bent over him and straightened, her own face whitening.

"You haven't touched anything?"

"No, Reverend Mother."

"Remain here. I will tell the others to stay in the recreation room, send Sister Margaret down to keep you company and then telephone the police. I fear the grand silence will have to be postponed tonight."

She sketched the sign of the cross over the boy and went out. Sister Joan knelt, automatically beginning to whisper the prayers for the dead while her mind wrestled with shock and outrage. Someone had carried the boy here, left him for the sisters to find when they came into chapel for evening prayers and the blessing. Who?

"Sister Joan, Reverend Mother just told me—oh, the poor child! Is this—?"

"Petroc Lee," Sister Joan said.

"Someone laid him here." Sister Margaret's round face was distressed. "I hope it was not done in mockery. Shall we pray, Sister?"

For a quicksilver lad who had swum and splashed in a willow-fringed pool, for a child of twelve whom someone had killed and brought here.

"Sister Margaret." The prioress had returned. "The police are on their way. I have informed the other sisters that a great tragedy has occurred and instructed them to remain in the recreation room in case they are needed for questioning. The prayers and blessing and subsequently the grand silence will be accordingly delayed. Will you brew some very strong sweet tea? I feel it may be beneficial. Oh, I have sent Sister Hilaria over to the postulants' house, to tell them to join the other Sisters at recreation. I fear it is necessary to bend the rules a trifle at a time like this."

"Yes, Reverend Mother." Sister Margaret hurried out,

with a last shocked and sorrowing glance towards the altar.

"Is there anything you want me to do, Mother Dorothy?" Sister Joan felt herself taut as an arrow, ready for flight.

"I think that you had better remain here until the police arrive. Then come to the parlour. I shall place it at their disposal. As you made the report your presence will doubtless be required."

Sister Joan nodded and sank again to her knees, bowing her head, waiting for shock to be transmuted into anger and grief. Grief for a young life cut short, anger against whoever had done this deed.

Outside, cars disturbed the quiet of the evening. She rose, turning to face the prioress who entered with two policemen. They passed her and bent over the still figure.

"We shall require photographs," the taller of the two said, lowering his voice slightly as if he paid tribute to the fact he was in a chapel. "I would like this section closed off until it has been thoroughly searched."

"The library and store rooms are above." Mother Dorothy indicated the spiral stairs by the Lady Altar. "The door that leads into the visitors' parlour is kept unlocked. It communicates with the garden and with the chapel. That door there by the confessional."

"Is it always kept unlocked?" There was a tinge of criticism in his tone.

"It has always been the custom, officer. This convent is remote and we have nothing of material value here. If anyone should seek the consolation of private devotion it is not for me to bar the doors against them."

"Maybe so, Sister, but not locking the door in this day and age is asking for trouble," he retorted.

"I am Mother Dorothy, not Sister. This is Sister Joan."

"You were down at the station earlier today. Making a report about the missing lad and having your fingerprints taken."

"Yes," Sister Joan said.

"And you found the body? Sis—Mother Dorothy, the quicker we start the quicker we can be finished. If you have a room you can make available—?"

"The parlour will suit your purpose, officer."

"Detective Sergeant Mill, Mother Dorothy." He pointed the correction delicately, gave the body a long, considering look and went out.

The two nuns followed, one small and upright in her grey habit, the other small and bent in the purple habit that denoted her position as prioress. She would remain as superior for another four years, possible nine years since it was permissible to serve two consecutive terms. After that she would be Sister Dorothy again, with only a purple ribbon to remind her of past authority. It was better to think of that rather than of the camera and fingerprinting equipment being carried through from the main hall as they went through to the parlour.

"This will do very nicely, Mother Dorothy." Detective Sergeant Mill gave the large room a glance of approval.

"I have asked our lay sister, Sister Margaret, to brew tea for everybody. The other sisters are in the recreation room with our two postulants in case you wish to call any of them."

"I'll probably have a word with them *en masse*," he said, settling at the prioress's desk.

"About the chapel—?" Mother Dorothy looked enquiring.

"We'll be finished there in about an hour. The body will be removed for examination. After that you can hold your prayers, whatever."

How quickly a living boy became a body. Sister Joan, catching a wincing look on the prioress's face, knew they shared the same thought.

Sister Margaret came in with a tray of tea, put it on the desk, and withdrew. Her eyelids were reddened as if she had shed a few tears. Sister Joan wished she could burst into tears, but her eyes were dry, her throat tight.

"I think it will be useful to begin at the beginning," Detective Sergeant Mill said, unscrewing a ballpoint pen and nodding to his fellow officer who did the same. Both men had taken out their notebooks. "I'd like the two of you to stay."

"Be so kind as to pour the tea, Sister Joan and then sit down." Mother Dorothy seated herself.

Doing as she had been bade, she concentrated on keeping her hands steady.

"This is the Order of the Daughters of Compassion?"

"Founded in 1942 by a laywoman called Marie Van Lowen, a Dutchwoman who was martyred at Dachau—the concentration camp," Mother Dorothy added.

"I've heard of it. How many convents are there?"

"Of this Order? Two in Holland and three in England and two in the mission field. We are not a large Order."

"Well, let's get a list of everybody in this convent. You're the prioress?"

"I am Reverend Mother Dorothy. I have been prioress for a year and have four more years to serve."

The other officer moved from his place at the end of the desk to murmur a few words in his senior officer's ear.

"I wasn't here then." Detective Sergeant Mill looked up again. "There was an—incident at this convent last year. My predecessor dealt with it. This isn't connected?"

"I am certain that it isn't, but you will be able to check the notes your predecessor made."

"Thank you, Mother." His tone was as dry as her own. "I shall require ages and surnames."

"We relinquish our surnames when we enter the Order," she said repressively. "We keep our baptised names unless they are wildly unsuitable. Age is surely a private matter."

"The boy was carried into the chapel." He tapped the end of his pen on the desk.

"Not by one of my community, Sergeant!"

"I hope not, Mother Dorothy."

"I am fifty-seven," she said. "As you may have noticed I have a bad back—disc trouble. I doubt if I could have carried him. The surnames you will have to wait to receive. It will be necessary for me to look them up."

"How many sisters are there here?" he asked.

"Apart from myself there are eight fully professed sisters, one who has not yet made her final profession, a lay sister and two postulants."

"Their names?" The pen was poised again.

"Sister David is our librarian. She is in her mid-thirties, small and short-sighted; she acts also as my secretary. She also translates manuscripts from the Latin as her contribution to the finances of the community. Each of our houses is self supporting."

"And Sister Joan here?" He nodded in her direction.

"I joined this community last year," Sister Joan said. "I'm thirty-six and I teach at the small school on the moors."

"Sister Perpetua is the infirmarian," the prioress continued. "Mid-forties. She has no external work since much of her time is occupied with caring for our two oldest members of the community. Sister Mary Concepta is in her late seventies and crippled with rheumatism, Sister Gabrielle in her eighties. They sleep down in the infirmary.''

"Retired."

"On the contrary we all benefit from their wisdom and advice. Nuns, unlike police officers, never retire.''

"And the others?" He ignored the gibe.

"Sister Martha is in her thirties. She takes care of the garden and sells what produce we ourselves don't eat. Sister Katherine is in her late twenties. She deals with the linen and earns her living by embroidering copes and altar cloths and the like. Sister Hilaria is in her early forties and our novice mistress.''

"You said there was one who hadn't taken her vows."

"Sister Teresa has taken her temporary vows. Provided the community agrees she will make her final profession—vows for life—next year. She is in her early twenties and makes herself useful where she is required.''

"I know Sister Margaret," the other office volunteered, speaking for the first time. "Lovely lady but drives like a bat out of hell—pardon me, Sisters.''

"Sister Margaret," said Mother Dorothy, acknowledging the apology with a slight inclination of the head, "is our link with the outside world. She attends to the housekeeping and does the shopping. You must understand that we are semi-enclosed, entering the world only when our work or circumstances render it absolutely essential.''

"You said that you had two—postulants?''

"Sister Elizabeth and Sister Marie—both in their twenties. They have taken vows for two years, the first of which is spent in strict seclusion largely in the novices' quarters which are in the cottage behind the old tennis court. They come to the main building only for prayer and instruction.

After a year they will move into the main building as Sister Teresa has done.''

"It sounds very structured." He gave her an approving smile.

"Yes, it is. A life strictly regulated so that the spirit might be free."

"If you'll excuse me, Sisters?" The other officer received a glance from Detective Sergeant Mill and rose. "I'll go and check on how things are progressing in the chapel."

As he went out Sister Joan exclaimed, "Mother Dorothy, someone will have to inform Padraic Lee! He's the child's uncle."

"That's being attended to, Sister. He'll be wanted for the formal identification. I understand he's been looking for the lad himself."

"They will all have been looking," Sister Joan said. "The Romanies care for their children."

"As do all decent folk." He looked suddenly more tired, more careworn. "I've two boys of my own so I know how—excuse me."

A raincoated man had come to the half open door and he went over to him, pulling the door close behind him, his conversation inaudible.

"Am I to open the school tomorrow, Mother Dorothy?" Sister Joan asked.

"I think it would be the best course of action, Sister."

"What about Kiki Svenson?" She lowered her voice to a whisper.

Mother Dorothy frowned consideringly. "For the moment it would be better to say nothing on that score," she murmured back. "It would be very irresponsible of us to direct attention to something that may have no relevance to what has happened. However, in view of the changed circumstances, I will telephone Sweden instead of writing. I believe the expense will be justified. Certainly I shall pray that our minds be set at rest in this matter at least.'' She broke off as Detective Sergeant Mill came into the parlour again.

''We've finished with the chapel and the rest of that wing, Mother. There's an ambulance on the way.''

''Are you permitted to tell us anything?'' Mother Dorothy asked.

''The doctor's made only a quick preliminary examination. The boy's been dead for about twenty-four hours—hard to be specific. Cause of death isn't clear yet—doctor says he would bet it was an overdose of something, but the contents of the stomach will have to be analysed before he can be certain. Oh, one other thing, the lad wasn't interfered with, if you know what I mean.''

''I am relieved to hear it,'' the prioress said. ''If it was an overdose then could accident be a possible solution?''

''Except that someone carried him into your chapel and laid him out neatly. Accident seems unlikely unless—but I'm delaying you, Sisters.''

''I have already said that we are at your disposal,'' Mother Dorothy reminded him.

''Very kind of you, Mother Dorothy. We shall be back in the morning to take any statements necessary from the sisters. I don't want to alarm them.''

''I very much doubt if anyone in the community will be able to provide you with any useful information, Sergeant, but I will ask the sisters to provide detailed written accounts of their movements during the last twenty-four hours, if that will help.''

''It will indeed, Mother Dorothy. Thank you.''

''I shall be going over to the school to teach tomorrow—as usual?'' Sister Joan glanced at him.

"Just carry on as normal, Sister. Oh, I've taken the liberty of having one of my men telephone the local parish priest—Father Malone? The boy was a Catholic, it seems. There was a rosary in the pocket of his jeans."

"Some of the people in the camp are Catholics," Sister Joan said. "I didn't know that Petroc was one. Romanies usually adopt the religion of wherever they happen to be, and this district is mainly Protestant so I would have thought—"

"He didn't mention it to you?"

She shook her head.

"Whenever there's a feast day all the Romany children claim to be members of the Church just so they can take advantage of the day off. Father Malone will know for certain."

"Yes, well—thank you again, Sisters. Goodnight." He unexpectedly thrust out his hand and shook hands with them both. "You'll be having to get your chapel reconsecrated or whatever, I suppose. After having the body there, I mean."

"The body of a child does not soil any place," Mother Dorothy said. "Goodnight."

Outside, cars were starting up. Going with the two officers to the door Sister Joan flinched as the light from headlamps illumined a stretcher being carried round from the side.

"Nasty business, Sister." The other officer sounded angry. "Always nasty when it's a child."

"Yes."

There was, she thought, nothing more to be said.

"I have asked Sister Margaret to invite the rest of the community down to prayers," the prioress said, coming towards her. "The grand silence has been delayed already and I feel strongly that we need silence now, so that what has happened may be put into perspective. Oh, and if you wish to visit the camp in order to offer your condolences you may do so without first coming to ask for permission.''

''Thank you, Reverend Mother.'' Sister Joan turned and went into the chapel wing. Nothing seemed to have been disturbed; the sanctuary lamp still burned with a steady blue flame; nobody lay before the altar. Then, slipping into her place, she noticed the seals on the doors leading to the visitors' parlour and the confessional. Evidently a more thorough examination would be made in daylight.

The others were coming in, silently, heads bowed. Only Sister Mary Concepta was grunting a little with effort as Sister Teresa shepherded her to her seat. Sister Joan wished it were permissible to turn her head and study the faces of her sisters. Was it possible that one of them had—but who? She let their faces pass across the surface of her mind as the prioress began the recitation of the rosary.

Not the old ladies and not the postulants who never went anywhere unsupervised. Not the prioress or delicate Sister Katherine who often needed help before she could lift the piles of heavy linen. Sister Martha looked frail too but she was wiry; Sister Hilaria had large, powerful hands—stop it, stop it at once. Someone from outside did this and then brought him here. Why? Why not simply bury him out on the moor? It might be years before anyone ever found him. Why bring him here to the convent?

''—as it was in the beginning, is now, and ever shall be,'' Mother Dorothy intoned. Hands raised, fluttered crosses in the soft lamplight.

''You are all aware that the missing child, Petroc Lee, was found here earlier this evening.'' The prioress was on her feet, facing them. ''The cause of his death has not been established, but it seems certain that he died about twenty-four hours ago and that someone brought the body here. The police have asked for statements. Someone may have seen something, some tiny detail they didn't consider important at the time. I wish the rising signal to be sounded half an hour early in the morning. You will all have had a night's sleep and will employ the extra time before coming into chapel in writing a brief account of your own memories of the last twenty-four hours. You will also be required to have your fingerprints taken, for elimination purposes. What has happened is very distressing, especially for Sister Joan whose pupil the child was. For the rest we will continue as usual. The tragic event must not be made an excuse for idle gossip and speculation. Sister Margaret, as it is so late you and Sister Joan will accompany Sister Hilaria and her charges to the postulants' quarters and return together."

"Please, Reverend Mother." Little Sister David had put up her hand. "You don't think someone might be—lurking?"

"No, Sister David, I don't think anything of the kind." Mother Dorothy sounded wearily impatient. "Sister Margaret and Sister Joan, you are excused from observing the grand silence until you re-enter the main house. Let us pray."

She lowered herself to her knees again, beginning to intone the prayer for the dead.

At the chapel door Sister Joan knelt briefly for the blessing, feeling the cool drops of water on her face as the Prioress sprinkled some from the aspergillum. Mother Dorothy was in shadow, only her eyes alive and troubled behind her rimless spectacles.

The five walked in silence through the garden and along the narrow path that led past the disused tennis court to the old dower cottage where the postulants lived under the gentle rule of their novice mistress. Sister Hilaria's face, still shrouded partly by her scarf, looked strained in the light from Sister Margaret's torch. The two white bonneted postulants walked close together. One of them let out a high-pitched nervous giggle and clapped her hands to her mouth.

The door of the postulants' quarters closed behind them. Turning, Sister Margaret said in a reassuring tone, "There was no need for you to accompany me, Sister. I am quite sure there is not the least danger."

"I rather think that Mother Dorothy was heaping coals of fire on our heads to remind us that we'd both broken the grand silence already this week," Sister Joan said wryly. "I, for one, am glad of the chance to say something no matter how trivial. Silence is so full of questions."

"That poor child." Sister Margaret sighed. "I have been trying to make sense of it. Why would anyone wish to harm a child? A little boy of twelve? You know, I could not help remembering how only the other evening we both stood and watched him playing and splashing with the other child. The old woman who spoke to us said there was evil, but it cannot have been in the children. I have been wondering if possibly someone else was also watching them, someone with a sick and twisted mind. It would have been possible."

"I have been thinking the same thing myself," Sister Joan said gravely.

"At least the child will be happy now." Sister Margaret's voice had brightened. "Our Dear Lord so loves to welcome children into His kingdom. Oh, there will be rejoicing there now."

"There will be anger," Sister Joan said flatly. "Our

Blessed Lord is hardly likely to be rejoicing because a child has been murdered, Sister.''

"Yes, you are quite right, Sister." The brightness had drained from Sister Margaret's face. "I had not thought of it yet in that light. I spoke without thought.''

"So did I. I didn't mean to snap your head off, Sister.''

"Oh, it takes a lot to do that," Sister Margaret said. "You were right, Sister, to chide me. My opinions are sometimes—naive, I fear, but they give me some comfort and I am inclined to cling to them. It is a matter of finding compensations in even the most stressful conditions. For you it must be a great grief since you were the child's teacher. We can only thank God for the rule of detachment from personal affections. At least you have that to lend you strength.''

Do I? Sister Joan asked the question silently of herself as she followed her companion up the path. Aren't the children becoming a substitute for me because I will never bear any of my own? Not much detachment there.

"I'll just lock the front door and check that Mother Dorothy doesn't want anything," Sister Margaret said, turning just before they entered the main building. "You get a good night's sleep now. I must remind myself not to talk. To break the rules seems to be becoming quite a habit with me, I'm afraid. As it is I shall have to confess that I've lost my rosary. It was loose on the chain and I delayed having it fixed. Most careless. Goodnight and God bless you.''

She and her torch passed within. Sister Joan opened her mouth and closed it before following. There were moments when keeping all the rules became an almost unbearable strain.

NINE

✠ ✠ ✠

Father Malone had offered mass and hurried away again after drinking a cup of tea in the parlour. Usually he came up to the refectory to enjoy a bit of a chat with the Sisters but this morning nobody was in the mood for light conversation. There was an air of strained solemnity among even the postulants who, having attended mass, were shepherded back to their quarters by a heavy-eyed Sister Hilaria.

"Sister Joan." The prioress stopped her as she was on her way downstairs. "I have asked Sister David to take your place at the school for a couple of hours. She prefers to walk over as you know so you can ride Lilith over later. I want you to read through the statements made by the community before the police arrive. It is possible that something in them might strike a chord with you."

"Yes, Mother Dorothy." She made the expected reply, fighting back a twinge of irritability. The pupils were her pupils and at a time like this would need their regular teacher. She doubted if Sister David would give them the sense of security they required in the face of the sad news to be imparted.

"Whatever work you are given to do, do it well and take pride in it, but always remember that you are first and foremost a religious," Mother Agnes had once instructed her.

The statements, her own among them, had been collected and lay in a pile on the desk, each one signed and dated. Seating herself she began the task of reading them. Those made by the postulants could almost be discounted. The two girls had been in their quarters apart from their attendance at mass. When Sister Hilaria had gone to the dentist Sister Teresa had gone over to supervise their studies. Sister Teresa's statement bore that out. On the previous evening she had cooked the supper since Sister Margaret had been driving Sister Joan to visit the parents. Nothing there of interest.

Both the elderly nuns had contributed, Sister Mary Concepta weaving little prayers for the dead child in between her assurances that she had spent her time as she always did between the infirmary and the chapel; Sister Gabrielle submitting a brief and concise timetable of her own movements which coincided with those of Sister Mary Concepta.

Mother Dorothy's own statement was equally brisk and matter-of-fact. Sister David had gone into more detail about the translation of Euclid she was working on for a college undergraduate; Sister Martha had taken advantage of the loosened soil after the rain to pull up some weeds; Sister Katherine and Sister Perpetua had changed the linen and looked after the old ladies between them. All the community apart from Sister Margaret, Sister Hilaria and herself had been within the confines of the convent, and nobody had seen anything out of the common.

She turned with heightened interest to Sister Hilaria's account.

On the night before last I began to suffer from toothache caused by the loss of a filling. Accordingly, after my charges were in their cells, I went to the chapel to offer up the discomfort in reparation. Reverend Mother Dorothy noticed the swelling in my cheek and instructed me to have the matter attended to on the following day. Accordingly I went into Bodmin, Sister Joan kindly driving me, and had my tooth extracted. Afterwards Sister Joan took me for a cup of coffee and while we were drinking it Mr. Padraic Lee came into the cafe to request that Sister Joan report the disappearance of his nephew to the police. He kindly offered to drive me back to the convent, which offer I accepted with gratitude. When I reached home I was still feeling a trifle dizzy from the effects of the injection and at Mother Dorothy's kind suggestion went to lie down in the infirmary. Oh, I neglected to mention that on the way into Bodmin we paused briefly at the old Druid house on the greenway to speak to one of Sister Joan's pupils and a young man employed in the child's family. I reminded myself that in many ways the fallen archangel Lucifer is most deserving of our pity, though we must never allow pity to degenerate into sentimentality. After supper, as I was feeling better, I settled my two postulants—excellent girls both of them—in their quarters and returned to join in the recreation hour with my sisters.

Sister Joan read the statement through again, frowned, and took up Sister Margaret's account, which read more like a gossipy letter than anything else.

On the evening before last I drove Sister Joan on a round of visits to some of the parents of her pupils. We visited Mr. and Mrs. Penglow whose son and daughter were also present and had a welcome that was most gratifying and spoke much for Sister Joan's success as a teacher. Afterwards we failed to find the Wesleys in but were given a splendid supper by Mr. and Mrs. Holt which was a great treat. Sister Joan went out to look at a baby calf but I did not. Though we practise vegetarianism in the Order there was a time when I enjoyed roast beef. I received some recipes from Mrs. Holt which I hope to try out for the community, and then we drove on to see Mr. and Mrs. Olive and their daughter who have moved into the district over the last couple of months.

Yesterday morning I awoke the community and prepared breakfast as I always do. After breakfast I loaded the water cans in the back of the car and drove over to the presbytery where I filled the cans and had them blessed by Father Malone—such a kindly priest and never out of temper. I then drove home and prepared the midday meal. Mother Dorothy told me that Sister Joan was to have the use of the car in order to drive Sister Hilaria to the dentist so I went out and gave the vehicle a bit of a polish. During the afternoon I wrote out the recipes that Mrs. Holt had kindly given me and put them into my cooking file; then I cleared up the kitchen and made some herb tea for Sister Mary Concepta who is permitted it as a remedy for the severe rheumatism that quite incapacitates her at times. I then went to my cell for the religious study period. I am reading the published journals of His Holiness Pope John the Twenty-Third—most interesting and giving great food for thought. Oh, I forgot to mention that just before that Sister Hilaria came home in Padraic Lee's lorry. I gave her a cup of tea and Mother Dorothy agreed with me that she should lie down for a couple of hours.

*Later Sister Joan returned, having accomplished the
journey without mishap, thanks be to Our Dear Lord.
After supper I washed up the dishes and joined the community at recreation.*

She hadn't mentioned losing her rosary. Sister Joan
wondered whether to mention it herself. She would wait,
she decided, since it was possible that Petroc had his own.
If not, then it was obvious he had found Sister Margaret's
and that meant he had been wherever she had dropped it.
Not, surely, in the Romany camp else she would have
discovered its loss sooner. That left the Penglows, the
Wesleys (since they had alighted from the car to make
enquiries of the neighbours), the Holts and the Olives.
She put the statement back on the file, added her own brief
account, and looked up as Mother Dorothy came in with
Detective Sergeant Mill.

"Detective Sergeant Mill wishes you to go with him to
the Romany camp," she said without preamble. "He feels
they might talk more freely if you are present. I have told
him that we will, of course, co-operate fully in the police
investigation."

"What about school?" Sister Joan enquired.

"Sister David is perfectly able to cope, Sister. You may
go now with the officer."

"Yes, Mother Dorothy." She knelt briefly, aware of a
flicker of amusement crossing the detective's face as he
picked up the statements. Probably he considered the convent courtesies impossibly medieval.

He had driven himself since the car was empty. At a
little distance two policemen and a policewoman were
unloading photographic and fingerprinting equipment
from a van.

"We've got your prints already, Sister." He held open

the door for her. "I take it that you've read through the statements and there isn't much in them to throw any light on the matter."

"Nothing tangible."

"Can you give me a rundown of a typical day in your Order? I haven't a clue how nuns actually spend their time." He thrust the pile of statements under the dashboard and positioned himself neatly behind the wheel. Early forties, she reckoned, and thinner than the popular image of the police with grey streaks in brown hair and disconcertingly shrewd brown eyes.

"Easily. We lead very regulated lives. We rise at five and go to the chapel as soon as we have washed our faces and cleaned our teeth—you want details?"

"If you please, Sister?"

"In chapel we have our individual private devotions until 6:30 when either Father Malone or his curate, Father Stephen, comes to offer mass. Then we go up to the refectory for breakfast—cereal, a piece of fruit, and coffee. We eat it standing. After that we sweep and clean our cells and then go to our respective duties. I teach in the local school, Sister David does translation work—she is a Latin scholar—Sister Katherine sells her embroidery and Sister Martha some of her garden produce, and Sister Margaret bottles fruit which she sells in the local market. We are all in our cells again by five when we pursue religious studies. We discuss what topic we wish to concentrate on with the prioress who supervises the progress of our work and sets essays and meditation reports from time to time. At six we go into chapel for further devotions and Benediction; then at 7:30 there is supper—"

"What happened to lunch?"

"Oh, a meal of soup and bread and fruit is served at midday. As I am still at the school I take an apple and a cheese roll. Sometimes I make hot soup for myself and the children when the weather is cold. At supper we have soup or a salad, then a main course of fish or cheese or something on toast and a pudding—steamed or milk. I can't see how all this is going to be the slightest help to you.''

"I'm building up a picture." He curved the car on to the moorland track.

"Well, during the meal one of the community reads aloud from a book about one of the saints or something of that nature. She eats her meal later and we take turns at reading. After supper we have an hour's recreation when we sit round with our work—knitting and mending and talk. Mother Prioress sometimes joins us, also Sister Hilaria. At 9:00 we go down to the chapel again for evening prayers and then we receive the blessing and after that there is the grand silence.''

"Do you," he enquired, "get time off at the weekend?"

"On Saturdays I help Sister Martha in the garden and prepare lessons for the coming week. On Saturdays we have general confession over which Mother Dorothy presides, and we make our private confessions to Father Malone or Father Stephen on Wednesdays. On Sundays we have an extra hour of recreation during the afternoon. If it's a nice day we walk in the garden. We also borrow books from the library which is extensive or write letters home.''

"Absolute regularity, obedience, sexlessness—how do you stand it?" he enquired.

"We all chose it," Sister Joan said, flushing slightly.

"A pretty woman like you ought to be happily married with children." He sounded angry as if her choice of the religious life were a reflection on his masculinity.

"Marriage is a vocation too," she argued. "I just didn't happen to choose it."

"You didn't mention flagellation." His voice challenged her.

"These days that particular penance is merely symbolic. Oh, and we don't wear hair shirts or stick pins into ourselves either. And I'm terribly sorry to disappoint you but there isn't a lesbian, a transvestite or a child molester in our entire community."

"Temper, temper, Sister Joan." He shot her a glance too teasing for her peace of mind.

"I beg your pardon. It's only that I get a bit weary of the misconceptions we come up against sometimes," she said stiffly.

"Fed up," he substituted.

"Exceedingly fed up, Detective Sergeant Mill."

"Here's the camp." He slowed the car and stopped. "The pathologist's report is in. The boy died of a massive overdose of LSD, taken by mouth in what seems to have been a bottle of wine. Have you any ideas about that? Your pupils aren't junkies by any chance?"

"No, of course not. The notion is absolutely ridiculous. Drugs? It seems—bizarre."

"In this rural district apart from the odd spot of glue sniffing and a few hopefuls who think they can get away with growing marijuana in their back gardens we haven't had much trouble in that area," he said. "Of course the Romanies may deal in drugs."

"They deal mainly in scrap metal. Even if one or two of them are—they'd never give it to a child, especially one of their own."

"He might have got hold of it by accident."

"Then how did he come to be in the chapel?"

"You're right, of course. He was carried in, probably

through that damned unlocked side door, and arranged neatly while the rest of you were at your recreation. From now on I'm going to insist that the entire building is locked at night. Anyone in need of spiritual comfort can ring the bell like ordinary people. Shall we get out here and walk?''

"I hope my being with a member of the police force isn't going to ruin my reputation,'' she said, getting out of the car.

"Don't worry, Sister. I'll make it clear you're not under arrest.''

"They are more likely to mistake me for a copper's nark,'' she countered.

They were approaching the semi-circle of wagons, passing the willow trees through which the dull gleam of water could be seen. Petroc had swum and splashed here in the cool evening, unaware that he had only another day to live. Her eyes filled with tears and she blinked them rapidly away, swallowing hard.

The men were still sorting scrap; washing hung on the lines; a baby was crying in one of the wagons; a dog barked. Everything seemed as usual but she sensed a darkness over the camp. The school would only be half full, she realized, seeing her four pupils in a neat and unnaturally silent group on the steps of the Smith wagon. Tabitha and Edith, wearing black cotton pinafores over their jeans and sweaters, sat together on the bottom step. Above them Hagar and Conrad occupied separate steps, the boy having a black band round his arm, Hagar's long hair tightly plaited and looped under a black headsquare.

"Good morning, children.'' She heard the false brightness of her own voice and winced. "Sister David went into school this morning and I came over with Detective Sergeant Mill to see how you all were. This must be a sad day for you, so we must try to help by trying to remember anything useful to the police.''

''We don't know noth—anything,'' Conrad said.

''Hagar? You saw Petroc the evening before last, didn't you?'' She squatted down near the steps. ''You spoke with him and he said he was going somewhere. Can you remember exactly what was said? It might help.''

Hagar closed her eyes briefly, screwing up her forehead, then opened her eyes and said flatly, ''No.''

''You had had an argument with your brother—''

''I told her she ought to help out more now that Dad's done a bunk—run off,'' Conrad said.

''I went off in a temper,'' Hagar said, evidently deciding to open up. ''I went down to the pool. Sometimes Petroc and I like—liked to swim there and fool about. It was coming on to rain. Petroc was there, throwing pebbles into the water. I told him it looked like rain and he said, 'Well, I'll soon be under cover,' and then he ran off.''

''But not towards his wagon?''

''Out towards the moor.'' Hagar gestured vaguely. From under their slanting lids her black eyes conducted a close survey of the detective who stood a few feet away.

''Children, has anyone offered you any grass, hash, that kind of thing recently?'' he asked.

They looked at one another and shook their heads, only Edith piping up, ''I've been making a basket out of grass for the project, Sister.''

''Not that kind of grass, pet,'' Sister Joan said. ''Well, if you do remember anything at all you'll tell me or Detective Sergeant Mill, won't you? We want to find out what happened to Petroc. Where is Mr. Lee—your daddy, Tabitha?''

''He went into Bodmin to see about the funeral.'' It

was Conrad who answered. "He's swearing to kill anyone responsible."

"Sometimes we all say things we don't mean when we're very shocked or grieved," Sister Joan began.

"He means it," Conrad said. "We won't be coming to school until after the funeral on Saturday. Is that all right, Sister?"

"Yes, of course. I'll see you on Monday then. Try not to be too sad." Her voice trailed unhappily away. Glib words of reassurance would have splintered on the air.

"We didn't make much headway there," the detective commented as they walked away. "Well, it was worth a try."

"If Petroc was going to meet someone—someone he considered a friend—then he would have drunk a glass of wine unsuspectingly, wouldn't he?"

"The wine had been heavily sugared according to the pathologist. Probably it was too sour for his taste."

"And then in a little while the drug would have worked and he'd have gone tripping off into some fantasy world and died there." She shuddered.

"He had what's known as a good trip at any rate," Detective Sergeant Mill told her. "His expression and attitude were both serene."

"Because there were no devils in his subconscious. Do you want to speak to anyone else?"

"We can call in at the school. One of the others might have recalled something."

Assenting, she walked back to the car. The rhythm of the camp had not altered but she knew their visit had been noted.

"The boy was baptised a Catholic by the way," her escort said, opening the car door for her. "Seems he didn't keep it up, but he'll be buried as a Catholic."

"I forgot to ask." She bit her lip in annoyance.

"Ask what?"

"The rosary that was in his pocket. What was it like?"

"Just beads strung together. The chain joining them was snapped."

"Beads like this?" She held up her own rosary.

"Exactly like that. Perfectly ordinary beads."

"No, Sergeant. Most people have crucifixes on their beads that are made of silver or gold, sometimes rolled gold. The Daughters of Compassion have copper crucifixes. And one of our community lost her own rosary quite recently."

"Which sister?" He had set the car in motion.

"Our lay sister, Sister Margaret. She drove me round when I was visiting the parents. She only discovered its loss yesterday. She had a lot of work to do, going to fetch the holy water from the presbytery. We don't tell our beads until the evening."

"Does she mention it in her statement?"

"No, I don't suppose she thought it had any bearing on the matter. She mentioned it to me. She must have lost it the previous evening or she would have discovered the loss. Oh wait. That isn't right. It can't be. At the final evening prayers we say the rosary so she would have realized that the rosary wasn't there on the night before last. She might have lost it yesterday morning. At the presbytery."

"By which time Petroc Lee was already dead. So how did it come to be in his pocket?"

"I don't know. You'll have to ask Sister Margaret. She may have remembered by now."

"Wouldn't it have made a tinkling noise as it fell?"

"Not necessarily; not if she were standing on carpet or

grass. Sergeant, it really is no use asking me about it. Ask Sister Margaret.''

"I intend to," he said grimly.

"And don't go frightening her to death," she added. "Sister Margaret is a good, simple soul who won't tread on an insect if she can avoid it. If you start—grilling her she'll just get vaguer and vaguer and more and more confused.''

"You paint me as a dreadful bully, Sister," he commented.

"I just think that you don't understand how religious women function.''

"But I'm fairly experienced where women are concerned. Ask my wife.''

"Your private life," she said stonily, "is none of my concern. Why do you keep trying to muddle me?''

"Maybe I want a spontaneous reaction and not the expected one drummed into you by the convent training, Sister. But don't fret about Sister Margaret. I'll handle her with kid gloves. Here's the school. You can ask the other children about the rosary.''

Sister David's rather pretty singing voice stopped in mid chord as they entered. The five pupils present stood up, their expressions sharpening as they saw the detective with Sister Joan.

"Good morning, Sister. I was just trying to get a little singsong going—nothing disrespectful,'' Sister David began nervously, her rabbit nose twitching furiously.

"You sound splendid, Sister," Detective Sergeant Mill said genially. "Sister Joan is giving me a bit of a helping hand this morning. Sit down, children. Sister and I are trying to find out how Petroc met his death. You've already been told about that?''

"I broke the news to them," Sister David said. "Mother Dorothy advised it."

"Well, now—where shall we start?" He looked round. "Did anyone see Petroc the night before last? Between eight o'clock and midnight?"

There was a general shaking of heads.

"Why eight?" Sister Joan enquired in an undertone.

"That was roughly the time that Hagar Smith saw the lad," he replied. "Now I want you all to think very carefully. Has Petroc talked to you about any special friends he'd made recently? Anyone he'd arranged to meet?"

Again there was a bewildered shaking of heads.

"Did Petroc mention having found something? A rosary?" Sister Joan interposed.

"He didn't say anything to me," Timothy Holt said.

"So none of you knows anything?" The detective's smile was disappointed.

"The farm children and the Romanies don't mix very well together," Sister Joan murmured. "There's a deep-seated prejudice that divides the two communities. I do my best but children often reflect the attitudes of their parents."

"And you all know where you were the evening before last?" Detective Sergeant Mill pursued.

"Madelyn and I were at home watching the television," David Penglow said. "You saw us, Sister."

"You didn't go out after the sisters visited?"

"It still gets dark quick," Madelyn said virtuously. "We're not allowed out after dark."

"I was helping Dad muck out when Sister Joan came with Sister—Margaret?" At Sister Joan's nod he continued, "When they left I went back into the barn—we've got a new calf there. I went to bed quite early."

"I didn't," Billy Wesley informed them. "I stayed up

late and had fish and chips. We all went to the pictures earlier on—the whole family. Mum says she's sorry she missed you, Sister.''

Sister Joan who gravely doubted the happy-go-lucky Mrs. Wesley had said anything of the kind smiled slightly.

''What about you, Samantha?'' Detective Sergeant Mill glanced at his notebook.

''The two sisters came,'' Samantha said, standing up politely. ''After they went I had some supper and read for a bit and then I went to my room.''

''If you do remember anything then tell Sister here. We want to find out all about everything. You don't ever smoke or drink or use drugs, do you?''

Five blank faces stared back at him. Five heads were slowly shaken.

''Well, that's all for the moment.'' He sounded rather at a loss. ''Sister Joan.''

''Will you be able to manage here until teatime, Sister David?'' she lingered to ask. ''I'll ask if Sister Margaret or I may pick you up in the car, if you like.''

''Oh no, I shall enjoy a pleasant walk back across the moor,'' Sister David said quickly.

''If you're sure. The Romany children won't be back in school until next week, so you'll have a peaceful time anyway.''

''And the others are being very good. I expect,'' Sister David said, walking with her to the door, ''that the news about Petroc shocked them. I did break it as gently as I could, and we said some prayers.''

''The children have been unnaturally angelic all term,'' Sister Joan said. ''How did they take the news anyway?''

''Madelyn Penglow cried and Billy Wesley wanted to know if there was a maniac about. The others were too shocked to say very much at all. Is there any further news,

Sister? I realize one ought not to become involved but—''

"Why not?" The colour had flamed in her cheeks. "Why shouldn't we get involved, Sister David? A child has been killed and left in our chapel! Don't we have a duty to get involved?"

"I only meant—yes, of course, it is a terrible tragedy. In our chapel."

"Anywhere, Sister. Anywhere. I'll see you later." Closing the door, returning to the car, she thought for the first time that Sister David, for all her classical scholarship, was really rather a silly woman.

"My clever idea doesn't seem to have worked," Detective Sergeant Mill observed wryly, starting up the car. "I was hoping the children would open up more when they saw you with me, but it looks as if they don't know anything. My men are instituting house to house enquiries in the district. There'll be an inquest next week. Do you fancy a cup of coffee?"

"Very much but Sister Margaret will give you one when you drop me off at the convent."

"Ask permission," he gibed.

"It wouldn't be forthcoming, Sergeant. Shall we drive back then? I'm sure that there is plenty of work waiting for you at the station."

"As you please, Sister Joan." He trod hard on the accelerator, sending the car shooting forward. "I hope you're not offended."

"I take the invitation as a compliment, Sergeant," she told him demurely. "I was wondering—if it wouldn't be an imposition—I could ask Sister Margaret about when she lost her rosary. If the police start questioning her she will get completely muddled."

"Ask her and then ring me with the results. I take it that you're allowed to pick up a telephone?"

"With permission. Sister Margaret or Mother Dorothy take outside calls. Do you think that we'll find out who did this?"

"I hope so, Sister. I shall be staying on the case until we get results anyway. As I told you the death of a child is an abomination. I've two lads of my own."

He was serious again, his voice empty of feeling or rather—tight with feeling unexpressed.

"I'll take a rain-check on that cup of coffee. Try to have a chat with Sister Margaret as quickly as you can. Thank you for your help."

But she had not, she thought going inside, been very helpful at all. She had not even been completely candid with him. She hadn't mentioned the other incidents that had recently disturbed her—the missing candles, flowers and holy water, the unnatural goodness of the children, the macabre little verse Samantha had written, the sudden disappearance of Kiki Svenson . . .

"There you are, Sister. I have telephoned the Svensons but nobody appears to be in." Mother Dorothy stood at the door of the parlour.

"Are you going to try again, Reverend Mother?"

"In an hour or two. Since you are not teaching today you can help Sister Margaret with the meal. Will the police be requiring your assistance again?"

"I don't know, Mother Dorothy. I don't think so."

"Then go and make yourself useful in the kitchen, Sister. We have all been greatly discomposed this morning by having our fingerprints taken. One would like to get back into the normal routine as quickly as possible."

Nodding briskly she went back into the parlour and closed the door.

TEN

✠ ✠ ✠

"I'm so sorry, Sister, but I just cannot remember where or when I lost it." Sister Margaret looked distressed. "It is very good of you to wish to help me find it, but the fault of carelessness is entirely mine."

"The point is, Sister, that Petroc had a rosary in his pocket when he was found in the chapel which corresponds exactly to yours, with the chain snapped."

"Sister Joan, you can't think that I had anything to do with the death of that poor boy!"

"No, of course I don't," Sister Joan said warmly. "Petroc evidently found it and put it in his pocket. If you can recall where you lost it then his last movements can be more accurately pinpointed."

"But if I knew exactly where I lost it then it wouldn't have been lost," Sister Margaret said. "I mean I'd have noticed it fall and picked it up."

"If Petroc did find it and pick it up himself, then you must have lost it two nights ago when we were visiting the parents, but surely you'd have noticed it was gone when we had evening prayers."

An awkward flush stained the lay sister's round face.

"Not necessarily, Sister," she said in an embarrassed fashion. "This is a dreadful admission to make but by the time we get to evening prayers I am generally too tired to concentrate on them. I very often have a little nap, you see. I am doubly at fault since I have never spoken of it in general confession, but it is such a shameful weakness. The point is that I might have lost my beads during the evening and in that case the poor child must have picked them up, or I could have lost them yesterday morning. I simply don't know and the more I think about it the more confused I get."

"Could you tell Reverend Mother about it?" Sister Joan asked. "The detective sergeant asked me—well, I volunteered, but it amounts to the same thing. If you tell Mother Dorothy then she can ring up the station. You'll want your rosary back?"

"Yes indeed, though my carelessness in losing it suggests to me that I really don't deserve to have it," Sister Margaret said miserably. "I'll go and tell her at once."

"Is there anything else you want me to do?" Sister Joan looked round the kitchen where they had just finished washing the dishes.

"Could you possibly go and check up on Sister Gabrielle? She would insist on going out to sit in the garden and I fear the air is still a trifle fresh. An extra blanket might be appreciated."

"Yes of course. Where is she?"

"In the cemetery," Sister Margaret said. "Believe me but it wasn't my choice. She insisted on having her chair put there."

"Each to her own taste. I'll take a blanket out."

Leaving Sister Margaret to what was going to be an embarrassing interview with the prioress, she nipped up to the linen cupboard, took out a blanket, and went down into the grounds again.

The walled enclosure with its two rows of plain wooden crosses where past members of the community slept their eternal sleep was near the old tennis court. Sister Gabrielle, a rug tucked about her knees, sat in a cane chair, chin cupped in her hands as she contemplated the graves. She gave a slight start as the younger woman arrived at her side and fumbled to turn up her hearing aid.

"Gracious, Sister, you do creep about so!" she exclaimed.

"I'm very sorry, Sister Gabrielle. I didn't mean to startle you but Sister Margaret thought you might need another blanket."

"If Sister Margaret had her way I'd be positively suffocated with blankets. A dear, good soul but a terrible fusspot! Well, well, child, drape it around me. I can consider it as a penance, I suppose."

"Are you sure you want to sit here?" Sister Joan asked, lingering. "Wouldn't you feel more cheerful somewhere else?"

"On the contrary, Sister, I feel exceedingly cheerful here. Why shouldn't I?" The other gave a sudden impish grin. "After all I'm still sitting up, and at nearly eighty-five that's cause for congratulation, don't you think?"

"Everybody says that you're wonderful for your age, Sister."

"If I make it to ninety I'll be even more wonderful," Sister Gabrielle said. "I have been thinking about the child who was found in the chapel. Is it known yet how he died?"

"From a massive overdose of LSD in white wine with a lot of sugar added."

"Then it was murder," Sister Gabrielle said thoughtfully. "I have been hoping there might be some other explanation, but there couldn't be. Someone must have tempted him to drink the stuff and then carried him into the chapel when he was dead. There is something very sick and twisted about that."

"The police are being very thorough in their enquiries."

"And you're assisting them? I saw you prancing off with that good-looking officer this morning."

"Sister Gabrielle, I wasn't prancing!"

"Like a child let out of school," Sister Gabrielle said firmly. "That dream you had the other night—it could have been the prelude to temptation."

"Sister, I'm a nun vowed to chastity," Sister Joan said coldly.

"You think words spoken even to God can change the urges of the body and the wishes of the heart? You have a long way to go in the religious life, Sister."

"Are you saying that I have mistaken my vocation?" Sister Joan asked.

"On the contrary I am saying that you must have a very strong vocation otherwise you wouldn't be tempted," Sister Gabrielle said firmly. "Don't imagine that you are immune from feelings, my dear. The trick is to divert them into the proper channels, not to deny them. Are you still conscious of the presence of evil? I know that I am."

"So many unconnected things are happening," Sister Joan said worriedly, "and yet I have the feeling they are connected. Sister, do you see any links between a classful of children who suddenly start behaving like angels, candles, flowers and holy water disappearing from the chapel and a boy who dies of an overdose of drugs which all my instincts tell me were given to him?"

"I understand you went to see the parents on two nights running. What was your impression of them?"

"Mixed." Sister Joan smiled her thanks as the other thrust the extra blanket towards her. "May I sit on the grass, Sister?"

"Much more sensible than crouching down like a dormouse," Sister Gabrielle said. "The parents."

"Padraic Lee's wife has a drinking problem and I get the impression that he holds that family together. He takes good care of his two little girls and he takes—took care of his nephew, Petroc. Petroc's father is in gaol for a minor offence and his mother ran off. The father of the two Smith children, Conrad and Hagar ran off too—not with Petroc's mother, and Mrs. Smith does her best to cope but finds it hard. Those are the ones from the Romany camp."

"And the others? Farming people?"

"Not the Wesleys. They live on the edge of town and Billy's father is in and out of work like a yo-yo. They're good-natured and feckless. The Penglows and the Holts are farmers. The Penglows are conventional and rather dull; the Holts are quite elderly and had Timothy after Mrs. Holt had a series of miscarriages. Mr. Holt told me that he felt the presence of evil. I'd almost forgotten that! He's not the fanciful sort at all but a very down to earth working farmer."

"Close to the earth and sensitive to its vibrations. Is that it?"

"There are the Olives, newcomers who've bought the old Druid house. Their daughter, Samantha, comes to the school. They don't seem to be doing any farming. Mr. Olive is writing a book, I was told. He's slightly lame by the way. His wife is rather elegant. Oh, they had a Swedish au pair girl who left suddenly in the middle of the night, according to Samantha. Mother Dorothy is trying to contact her. If she fails then we will mention it to the police. Anyway they have a new au pair now, a very beautiful young man who doesn't speak English.''

"It sounds rather odd," Sister Gabrielle said. "You know the religious persuasions of the families?''

"The Lees are nominally Catholic—at least Petroc was, but they don't practice the Faith. The Holts are Catholic. The Penglows are Church of England and the Wesleys are too, though I don't think they go to church very often. I don't know about the Olives. You know the school is non-denominational. I try not to make distinctions.''

"You pussyfoot around, no doubt," Sister Gabrielle said with asperity. "All this modern tolerance is very well in its way but it has its dangers. In the old days we did at least recognize the boundaries. Is it possible that the child was killed by a passing stranger? No, I suppose not. He must have known his killer well enough to sit down and drink a glass of wine with him.''

"There is another thing, Sister Gabrielle. Sister Margaret lost her rosary somewhere and it was found in Petroc's pocket. If she lost it when she was out with me then that can only mean that Petroc was there later, and picked it up.''

"Or someone else picked it up and put it in his pocket.''

"And brought him to the chapel.''

"Presumably by car. How many of the families have cars?''

"Padraic brings the Romanies in his pick-up lorry. Mr. Holt brings Timothy and picks up Billy on the way—the Wesleys don't have a car so Billy walks part way, when he bothers to arrive at school at all, that is. The Penglows come by car and Samantha too. The au pair drops her off. Wouldn't we have heard a car?''

"Not if it was left at the gates and the—whoever walked

round to the side door. Presumably he knew our routine
and also that the door into the visitors' parlour would be
unlocked.''

"And that includes just about everybody in the district.
You see what a puzzle it is?''

"I see that a child has died before his time," Sister
Gabrielle said bleakly. "You know, I was sitting here before, warming myself in the spring sunshine, feeling happy
to be alive, yet thinking of that child who will never be
able to do what I was doing. We must pray for guidance,
Sister. I am convinced that the solution will be found. The
solution has to be found if God is to prevail. Now I shall
have a little nap, so you may tuck that wretched blanket
around me and go and find something useful to do.''

She switched off her hearing aid and closed her eyes
with finality. Sister Joan shook a sprinkling of grass from
the blanket and tucked it around the bony old frame. She
wondered if one day she would sit here and have a younger
sister perform the same task on her behalf. There was a
quiet continuity in that which was comforting. Then, with
shocking clarity, the detective sergeant's face loomed in
her mind, his voice mocking her, "I don't know how you
can stand it, Sister.''

She clutched her own well-fingered rosary and sped
back towards the convent.

"Mother Dorothy was most understanding about the
very careless way in which I lost my rosary," Sister Margaret said happily, turning a rosy face from the cooker as
Sister Joan entered the kitchen. "She was also very kind
about my habit of napping at the end of the day. She reminded me that Saint Therese had had the same habit and
had reached the conclusion that there were times when
Our Dear Lord wished her to have a little rest. Isn't that
comforting? Though that doesn't mean that I won't try

very hard to stay awake in future. She has rung the station and the rosary will be returned to me. Now I must try very hard to recall exactly where I dropped it.''

"If you strain too hard to recall something you generally don't succeed," Sister Joan said. "Why not forget about it and then the answer might pop into your head."

"That's excellent advice, Sister. I shall take it. Now I must get on and finish the baking. Both Sister Hilaria and I are excused from recreation this evening. Mother Dorothy feels it will do the postulants no harm to learn how to cook a decent meal, so they are to come over to the kitchen after supper for a lesson in the art of convent *haute cuisine*. Doesn't that sound grand?''

"What would you like me to do, Sister? I'm at your disposal,'' Sister Joan asked.

"Oh, Reverend Mother wishes to see you. I almost forgot about it,'' Sister Margaret said. "Something about a telephone call, she said. You had better go at once. Now where did I put the flour?''

"You wanted me, Reverend Mother?'' Tapping on the parlour door, entering and briefly kneeling, she was struck by the irrelevant thought that so many of the courtesies of the religious life might be construed as medieval by the modern world. How begin to explain that she and the others knelt not to the prioress herself but to the Christ her position represented in the community.

"I managed to get through to Sweden. In fact the cleaning woman answered. She spoke a little English, sufficient to inform me that Mr. and Mrs. Svenson are on holiday for the next ten days, and that their daughter, Kiki, was in England. I thanked her and left my name and the convent number. At the moment we are in a cul-de-sac as far as that line of questioning is concerned. I see no point in mentioning the matter to the police until we know a little more ourselves.''

"But surely—" Sister Joan began.

"To do so would be to raise suspicions and cast doubts when we have no logical reason for doing so. I would prefer you to talk again to the child—Samantha, draw her out a little. It might even be necessary for you to pay a second visit to her home. Sister Margaret will accompany you. If anything further is said that justifies my taking action then I will do so."

"Yes, Reverend Mother."

"Sister Margaret cannot remember where she lost her rosary which is a pity but one cannot force these things. She had noticed the links in the chain were weak but, mindful of our vow of holy poverty, had delayed reporting the matter."

The words "false economy" hovered in the air but were not spoken.

"I rang up the police station and spoke to Detective Sergeant Mill. He undertook to return the rosary to Sister Margaret, and said that your help had been invaluable to him."

"I doubt if it was," Sister Joan said. "He was merely being polite."

"I told him that if he required your assistance again you had my permission to co-operate in any way he deemed necessary."

"Yes, Reverend Mother." Sister Joan wondered if it would do any good at all to ask that she be excused from any such co-operation. Probably not.

"Not a very respectful or religious man," Mother Dorothy was continuing, "but it is always a mistake to judge a book by its cover. Possibly contact with our community will be of benefit to him. The study period is almost upon us. Are you meditating on the four branches of the rule? An essay at some future period might be of help to Sister Hilaria for her postulants. She is often short of new material.''

"Yes, Reverend Mother."

"I suspect," said Mother Dorothy unexpectedly, "that you find it strange I should have retained so unworldly a person as novice mistress."

"She isn't very practical," Sister Joan said, startled into candour.

"Sister Hilaria lives already half in the next world," Mother Dorothy said. "It is of inestimable benefit to the postulants to be exposed to such holiness early in their religious lives. It is also of benefit to Sister Hilaria to have the company of lively young girls whose problems and personalities tie her more closely to earth. She has the gift of reading souls, Sister Joan, a rare and valuable accomplishment in the religious life. Stand a postulant—stand anyone in front of Sister Hilaria and she will tell you the innermost heart of that person. And she is completely modest about it, believing that any of us could do the same with a little effort. So an essay from you will help her in her duties. Now you had better get to your studies. Tomorrow is Saturday so you will have the weekend in which to concentrate on your spiritual duties."

"Yes, Reverend Mother. I was wondering—" Sister Joan hesitated. "Is Petroc to be buried on Monday? If so then it would be a mark of respect to close the school."

"I have already asked Detective Sergeant Mill to inform the parents there will be no school on Monday, the day of the funeral. You and I will attend the requiem—also Sister David who has connections with the school since she was the teacher there before you joined us. Father Stephen is very kindly giving us a lift as

Father Malone will be conducting the service. Oh, the child's father will be there. Detective Sergeant Mill informed me that he had, as he termed it, pulled a few strings and the man's sentence is to be commuted immediately on compassionate grounds.''

"That was very nice of him!''

"As I said we ought not to judge a book by its cover. Thank you, Sister.''

Sister Joan collected some paper from the library and went to her cell. Writing an essay for the benefit of the postulants was a daunting task. How could she honestly explore her own thoughts and feelings when whatever she wrote would end up as instruction for the postulants? Her fingers ached for brush and palette, for the means to express her thoughts in vivid, living colours and shapes that leapt from the canvas.

"If I can't be the best then I won't settle for mediocrity,'' she had told Jacob.

"I'd say that made more sense than burying your talents completely in a convent,'' he'd answered.

"They won't be buried. Our skills will be used in the service of the community.''

"If the Mother Superior so decrees. So give up any idea of marrying me but don't stifle everything else in yourself.''

"I would marry you, Jacob, but you want your children to be Jewish and I'd want them to be baptised.''

"I want you to be happy,'' he'd said with the disarming gentleness that shook her resolve.

But her resolve had held, right through her lonely and doubt-ridden postulancy to the moment when, clad in white, she had lain spread-eagled before the flower-filled altar, making her vows, and not known until hours later that in the joy of that bonding she had not even paused to wonder if Jacob were present.

Chastity, she wrote swiftly, *is not confined to the celibate though the vow of chastity we take when we enter the religious life includes celibacy. But that celibacy need not be a barren denial of life. It can be the raising of our instincts into a freer, wider, more universal loving. Other women vow to love one man. We vow to love all mankind through the merits of—*

Mankind was Petroc, playing in the water, of the innocence of an adolescence that had been cruelly cut short. Mankind was someone who had arranged to meet that little boy and coldly, callously, given him his death potion. Her written words seemed glib and facile when she read them over.

Filing into chapel with the rest of the community at the end of the study period she noticed that Sister David was back. Evidently nothing untoward had happened in school. Indeed the day's activities and the long walk across the moor had brought a pink glow to the other's cheeks. It would be a courtesy to ask if Sister David might help out more often in the future. A way too of distancing herself from the children in preparation for the time when the school would finally be closed down and the pupils be allotted to schools in Bodmin.

Father Stephen had come to give Benediction. He was a tall, thin young man with, according to Father Malone, ambitions to end up as a bishop.

"Or a cardinal, God save us all!" Father Malone had said in his dry manner. "And the boy only just ordained. Optimism is a wonderful thing."

Father Stephen was reputed to be clever. Sister Joan reflected that it was more fitting that little Father Malone would be offering the requiem mass. Father Malone hadn't learnt any new theology since his training in the seminary as a young man, but his inarticulate sympathy with the bereaved and troubled savoured of more true goodliness. Hastily she reminded herself that it wasn't her place to criticize the local curate and bowed her head again.

Father Stephen departed, looking faintly relieved as he always did. She suspected that the overwhelmingly female aura of the convent discomposed him, unlike Father Malone who liked a bit of gossip when the service was over.

When this is all over, she decided, I will ask permission to spend the summer holidays in retreat.

Supper was spaghetti, a dish she had never much liked unless it were consumed in a trattoria with a bottle of good red wine. She wound the slippery strands around her fork and imagined lashings of pesto sauce while Sister Katherine finished the book about the Magdalene, her pretty face tense with nerves for of all things she dreaded her turn at reading aloud.

At recreation, the slow-growing knitting in her hand, she listened to Sister David rattling on about her day at the school—

"—really I had forgotten how tiring the profession is. But the children were very good. Quite apart from the present sad circumstances I am sure that Sister Joan has established discipline among them in a way that I never could."

Sister Joan hastened to disclaim the compliment. "They've been good ever since term began. If I knew the recipe for it I'd bottle it."

"Speaking of which—" Sister Perpetua leaned forward, reddish eyebrows working. "There is a rumour that after this evening's culinary demonstration the postulants are going to be let loose in the kitchen to cook the evening meal. I hope Reverend Mother can dispel the rumour else I shall have to lay in extra stocks of bicarbonate of soda.''

Her little joke made she uttered a sharp bark of laughter and was silent.

''The postulants may turn out to be very good cooks,'' Mother Dorothy said, smiling slightly. ''However you need not fret, Sister. They will help Sister Margaret only when their spiritual duties permit. Sister Katherine, your reading tonight was most eloquent. I find myself always so deeply moved by the recognition in the garden. Grief transmuted into the promise of resurrection.''

''I wonder if that poor child thought of that when he was dying,'' Sister Martha murmured, sounding unwontedly cross.

''The child's funeral is to take place on Monday,'' Mother Dorothy said, picking up the subject but ignoring the comment. ''Sister Joan and Sister David will accompany me to the requiem mass and to the funeral service. I think that on that morning private prayers for all the faithful departed should be the burden of our devotions.''

Conversation languished. It was difficult to make pleasant little jokes and sprightly conversation when the murder of a child hung on the air.

''It is time for chapel.'' Mother Dorothy folded up her own work and put it into the canvas bag. ''The grand silence has already been delayed on one evening this week. I'd not wish to repeat the fault.''

Hardly a fault, Sister Joan thought, putting away her own knitting with relief, since reporting the finding of Petroc's body couldn't be left until the following morning. At least Mother Dorothy hadn't mentioned that the grand silence had also been broken earlier on in the week.

''The battery's running out in my hearing aid,'' Sister Gabrielle was grumbling.

"I'll get it for you, Sister. Sister Teresa is helping Sister Mary Concepta," Sister Joan said.

"I can see that perfectly well," Sister Gabrielle enjoined her irritably. "That's why I mentioned it to you."

Sister Joan turned in the direction of the infirmary where the spare battery would be in Sister Gabrielle's locker.

Coming out with it in her hand she almost bumped into Sister Hilaria who was escorting her charges out of the kitchen. With their dark blue smocks and white bonnets they both looked like a pair of wooden dolls clad in peasant costume. From the kitchen the scent of baking wafted.

"We have been Marthas," said Sister Hilaria. "I fear that my cake didn't turn out very successfully—I beat the mixture for too long."

The postulants, cheeks scarlet from the heat of the oven and eyes lowered, had primmed up their young mouths, in an effort, Sister Joan suspected, not to giggle. She wanted to reassure them that giggling was not a mortal sin, but the rule forbade her to speak to them save under the most extreme necessity.

"Is it prayers already?" Sister Margaret emerged, pulling off her apron and looking flustered. "I am all upside down and back to front today. Sister Hilaria said something that suddenly caused me to remember—but it must wait until tomorrow."

"Sister Margaret!"

The lay sister had hurried past her, composing her face, anxious not to break any more rules.

"Remembered what, Sister?" Sister Joan persisted, catching her up in the corridor.

"The dirt and my broken beads," Sister Margaret hissed. "So clear now, and yet I still cannot believe—"

"When you are quite ready, Sister Margaret—Sister

Joan, we will begin evening prayers,'' Mother Dorothy said icily from the door.

And after the prayers the blessing and the grand silence folding them round. She had expected to dream but her sleep was empty of images, a peaceful blackness out of which she rose into the consciousness of morning.

Dawn or the middle of the night? Her senses told her the former but the sound of a rhythmic snoring from the cell next to her own hinted at the latter. She sat up and groped for her slippers and dressing-gown, padded to the door and opened it. The dim light from the corridor illumined the tiny hands of her fob watch. 5:15? No bell for rising had sounded which could only mean that Sister Margaret had spent rather too long chatting to her Dear Lord.

Another door opened further along the passage and Sister Perpetua stuck out her night-capped head, hissing, ''It's terribly late. Grand silence should have been over fifteen minutes ago. Run down and find out what on earth Sister Margaret thinks she is doing, if you please, Sister.''

Sister Joan tied the cord of her dressing-gown, adjusted her own night-cap, and went swiftly across the landing and down the staircase. Outside she could hear the first twittering of the birds.

''Sister Margaret?'' She risked a low call as she went along the chapel corridor. Not much of a risk, since from above she caught the sounds of other doors opening, of muffled whispers.

The chapel was empty. Having expected to see Sister Margaret there she paused, biting her lip. Above the altar the crucifix glowed softly in the light from the Sanctuary lamp. Flanked by—only one candlestick? What had happened to the other one?

A draught of air blew with sudden strength and the door leading to the visitors' parlour banged.

She crossed the chapel in two strides, wrenching open the door that should have been closed, almost tripping over Sister Margaret who lay, head at an unnatural angle, coif and veil half torn from her head, not moving. Never moving again.

ELEVEN

✠ ✠ ✠

"This seems to be getting to be a habit with you, Sister Joan." Detective Sergeant Mill spoke in a quizzical tone that didn't blend with the sombre atmosphere of the parlour where he sat at Mother Dorothy's desk with his partner at a side table. Raising indignant blue eyes she met his considering gaze and repressed the indignant reply on the tip of her tongue.

"Sister Joan went down to find out why Sister Margaret had not rung the rising bell," the prioress said coldly.

"At a quarter past five?" He consulted his notes.

Sister Joan nodded.

"You went immediately to the chapel?"

"Sister Margaret rose at about 4:30 and went into the chapel to pray before waking the community. I went in and noticed at once that a candlestick was missing from the altar. Then the door leading to the visitors' parlour banged. I opened it and—"

"The outside door was open?"

"Yes, but it was locked last evening. After evening prayers Sister Margaret went to lock it and then rejoined the rest of us as we filed out."

"The candlestick was on the altar during the evening prayers?"

"Definitely. We would have noticed immediately had it not been," Mother Dorothy said.

"The outer door showed no sign of having been forced," the detective sergeant said.

"There are two keys. I keep one myself and Sister Margaret had the other. As you know we have only just begun to lock the outer door at night. It doesn't appear," said Mother Dorothy with a note of gloomy satisfaction in her voice, "to have done any good."

"The only prints on the handle are those of Sister Margaret herself," he told them. "The key wasn't in the lock but apparently still on her key-ring."

"Which is attached to her belt by a fairly long chain," Mother Dorothy pointed out. "The keys were then slipped into her pocket. It wasn't necessary for her to detach any from the chain in order to open a door."

"And she would have opened the door if anyone had knocked for admittance?"

"I suppose so, but who would come knocking at the door before five in the morning?"

"The killer," he said bluntly.

"Coming to kill Sister Margaret—one of the other sisters? Why? What possible motive could there be?"

"Mother Dorothy, last night before we went into chapel for prayers Sister Margaret said that she had remembered—I took it to mean that she recalled where she had lost her rosary," Sister Joan said. "There was no time for her to say more. We were almost late for chapel. Oh, and she said something about having to think about it until the morning. But the—person who killed her couldn't have done so for that reason because I was the only one she said it to—"

She broke off abruptly, looking at him in dismay.

"At this stage," he said dryly, "I am not putting you very high on the list of suspects, Sister."

"There is another thing," she said hesitatingly. "I didn't mention it before since it didn't seem relevant. Things have been disappearing from the chapel—candles, some daffodils from a vase on the Lady Altar, holy water from the stoup. I went into chapel during the week and the crucifix was missing from the altar."

"Why on earth didn't you report it to me?" Mother Dorothy demanded.

"I came into the main building to do so, Reverend Mother, but you had just taken the postulants into the parlour for their instruction, so I came back into the chapel to wait and the crucifix was back on the altar. I told myself that I'd imagined it."

"I instruct the postulants on Monday afternoons," Mother Dorothy said.

"When did you notice the other things were missing?" he asked Sister Joan.

"I noticed there were no flowers in the vase early last Saturday morning. Sister Margaret was in the chapel at the same time and commented on the fact that there had been daffodils there the previous evening. I think it was then she mentioned that we seemed to be using candles at a tremendous rate. It was Sister Margaret's job to buy fresh supplies."

"And the holy water?"

"Sister David found the stoup empty on—Wednesday— yes, for she said there was sufficient for the blessing and Sister Margaret took the water cans over to the presbytery on Thursday morning."

He was making notes, his face absorbed.

"So someone was in the chapel on Friday night—

between the grand silence which begins at—9:30? and 4:30 when you and Sister Margaret were in the chapel; the same person, presumably, was there on Monday afternoon—at what time?''

''At 4:30. I rode Lilith home from school, had a brief word with Mother Dorothy, unsaddled Lilith and rubbed her down and went into the chapel to pray. It was just past 4:30.''

''Sister Hilaria had brought the postulants over from their quarters,'' Mother Dorothy confirmed.

''And school finishes?'' He glanced up.

''At 3:30 on a normal day—sometimes a little earlier or later. It takes me about half an hour to clear round, lock up and ride home.''

''So long? The school's only a couple of miles from here, isn't it?''

''I don't indulge myself with tearing gallops across the countryside,'' she said coldly.

''And the holy water would have been taken sometime before Wednesday evening. Did anyone notice how much water was left on Tuesday evening?''

''The aspergillum was full on Tuesday and almost full on Wednesday—it is used for Benediction and the blessing before grand silence, and refilled as necessary. There was a trace of water in the stoup. I recall thinking that Sister David must refill it.''

''From the cans?''

''Yes, but they were due to be refilled anyway,'' Mother Dorothy said. ''Usually Father Malone comes up to bless the water, but on Thursday morning he rushed off before Sister Margaret could ask him, so she drove over later in the morning to the presbytery.''

''That seems clear enough.'' He frowned at his notes. ''Mother Dorothy, I want you to ask your nuns to sit down and go back over the entire week in their minds. Did any of them notice anyone hanging round the convent? As the outer door to the visitors' parlour was kept unlocked the person must have entered through that way.''

''And that door is at the side, not overlooked by any windows other than the storerooms above the chapel wing. Anyone could have come and gone.''

''You didn't notice anyone following you home on Monday afternoon?''

Sister Joan shook her head. ''One or two cars passed me in the distance on the road beyond the moor. I didn't pay them any attention.''

''The community is in a state of grief and shock,'' Mother Prioress said. ''Will it be necessary for you to question them immediately?''

''Not if I can avoid it, Mother Dorothy, but make sure they start thinking hard about the events of this week. About Sister Margaret?''

''When the pathologist has made his report we shall expect her to be brought here to be laid in the convent cemetery,'' the prioress said. ''I have telephoned her parents and they will be here in a few hours. For the present Sister Teresa will take over the duties of lay sister, with help from the rest of the community.''

''I can have the bod—Sister Margaret brought back here by tomorrow evening.''

''The funeral will be on Monday. In the afternoon since Petroc Lee is to be buried in the morning, and both Sister Joan and Sister David ought to be present as well as myself. Thank you, Sergeant.''

''I doubt there'll be any surprises,'' he said, rising and beginning to collect up his notes. ''She was clearly killed by a blow to the temple with some heavy object. I'm hazarding a guess that when we find the missing candlestick

we'll have the murder weapon. Possibly she heard someone trying to get in at the side door, opened it and whoever
was there rushed past her, seized the first heavy thing to
hand and hit her with it as she was re-entering the door.''

"Her coif and veil were half off," Sister Joan said.

"Then possibly Sister Margaret was on her way through
the door and the other yanked her back by her veil and
struck her as she turned.''

"Sister Margaret was a plump woman," she frowned.
"She was physically quite strong.''

"Suggesting the attacker was a heavily built man. We
shall know more about that when we know the angle at
which the blow was struck. Meanwhile, Mother Dorothy,
please accept my condolences. I am treating the two deaths
as connected for the moment but there is also the possibility that they are not.''

"Sister Joan, please see the officers to the door,"
Mother Dorothy instructed.

On the front step Detective Sergeant Mill paused, waving his companion ahead. "I brought back the rosary.
Sister. No prints on it except Sister Margaret's. Not as
many of those as I'd have expected either. Looks as if
someone wiped it clean. Oh, and there are none of the
lad's prints on it either. So it was put into his pocket after
he died.''

"You had it mended." Taking it from him she held it
up.

"It was described and photographed in its original state
in case it ever figures as evidence. I reckon it's no use to
her now.''

"It will be buried with her, according to custom. Thank
you.''

"Sister." Nodding, he looked for a moment as if he

wanted to say something else, but instead turned and went down the steps towards the police car.

"Mother Dorothy." Turning back into the parlour she spoke abruptly. "May I use the car?"

"For what reason?"

"I want to go over to the school and check the place. Nobody thought of searching there, and there may be something—it's better than sitting still."

"You will have to make greater efforts to control your restlessness, Sister," the prioress said severely. "However it may yield some result. Please be back in time for study period."

"If I need to drive anywhere else—?"

"If you consider further driving absolutely necessary," Mother Dorothy said wearily, "then you have my permission, Sister. I would remind you that your first duty is to your sisters here."

"I thought of going to see the parents to tell them—"

"I imagine the police will do that if and when they consider it necessary."

"Yes, Reverend Mother."

Going out to the car, passing the kitchen where a red-eyed Sister Teresa was washing dishes, she felt her restlessness mount into impatience. If she could have talked to the parents perhaps an unguarded word, an expression inappropriate for the occasion, might have given her a clue that the police might miss. On the other hand her own efforts might well hamper them.

The school building looked as if it were crouching in its hollow with the green buds of the gorse springing around it. That, she reminded herself, would have to be cut back before much longer. A car was approaching, swerving nearer and stopping, as she alighted from the old jalopy.

"Sister Joan, glad I caught you!"

"Mr. Lee, what happened to the pick-up?" she enquired.

"Flat tyre, so Gideon Evans lent me this. Keeps it very nice, Gideon does, but I'm not at home in it so to speak. I was on my way to the convent. Someone told me there'd been police cars and an ambulance heading in that direction early this morning."

"I very much fear," she said gravely, "that the person who killed Petroc has—well, Sister Margaret was found dead this morning in the little corridor between the chapel and the visitors' parlour."

"I don't believe it." He spoke almost angrily. "Not Sister Margaret, not—why, she was one of the nicest women you could hope to meet. Sensible and understood how folk ticked—not a bit like a—begging your pardon, Sister. What happened?"

"We don't know yet. Apparently she opened the side door and someone rushed in and killed her."

"How? She was a bonny woman and would've fought back."

"She received a blow to the temple hard enough to kill her instantly. There is a candlestick missing from the altar—what is it, Mr. Lee?"

"A big silver candlestick? Heavy? With a square base and bits of wax in the top where a candle had been?"

"Yes. Have you seen it?"

"Not more than a couple of hours ago. I was taking a look through the scrap—a big pile of stuff was collected recently and with all the grief over Petroc nobody's sorted it out yet. There was a candlestick lying on top. My Tabitha said she'd seen it lying at the edge of the camp and put it on the pile."

"What did you do with it?" she asked urgently.

"I set Tabitha and Edith to polishing it," he said, looking anxious. "I was going to ask around because I'd have sworn it was good silver, but then the pick-up wouldn't start, and it went clean out of my head. I'd better tell someone or perhaps you'd—?"

"Mr. Lee, this time you have to make your own report," she said firmly. "The police have been very decent—releasing your brother before time—"

"As they should him being innocent and Petroc his only boy—all right, Sister, I'll drive straight into Bodmin and let them know."

"If someone else had thrown it on the scrapheap," she detained him to ask, "wouldn't the camp dogs have barked?"

"Them animals is always barking. Nobody pays them heed."

"I see. Mr. Lee, I was so sorry about Petroc."

"No sorrier than his killer's going to be when I get my hands on him." The dark face was grim. "You think the same person did in—killed Sister Margaret too? You ought not to be wandering about by yourself, Sister."

"Oh, I'm perfectly safe," she assured him. "Do go and report that candlestick now."

Unlocking the door, she stepped into the little hall with the cloakroom off at one side and the classroom ahead. With its chemical toilets which the Council emptied every other week, its wood-burning stove, its paraffin lamp to be lit only on the darkest winter morning it was a far cry from the technology of more modern schools but she had liked it the moment she had laid eyes on it the previous year. There was an air of cosiness about the long room with its two groups of desks, the swivel blackboard, the children's drawings tacked up on the wall. The familiar scent of chalk and polish hung on the air.

She moved from desk to desk, lifting each lid. The children usually carried their books to and from school and the shelves at the side held the supply of textbooks— all, she reflected, slightly out of date but when she had suggested buying new ones Mother Dorothy had demurred.

"We are not made of money, Sister. I am aware that Rhodesia is now Zimbabwe but the actual country is still in the same position on all the maps and you are at liberty to ink in corrections."

All the children had scratched their names on the inside lids of their desks. It was, she pondered, tracing the spindly capitals of Petroc with a sad finger, their way of staking out their territory. Even the Penglows had put their names. The great mystery was that no teacher ever caught them in the act of doing it. No, Samantha Olive hadn't inscribed her desk lid. No need to establish herself or no sense of identity? Whatever the reason only the names of previous pupils marked the smooth inner surface of the wood.

She went to the main desk from which she surveyed her class every morning and took out paper and pen. The list of questions unravelled from her hand.

(i) Who has been sneaking into the chapel to take candles, flowers and holy water and why?

(ii) Why have the children been so unnaturally good all term?

(iii) Where did Sister Margaret lose her rosary and what made her remember?

(iv) What "evil" did both old Hagar and Mr. Holt sense?

She crumpled up the paper and aimed it neatly into the wastepaper basket as the outer door opened and Detective Sergeant Mill walked in.

"I saw that old wreck your community laughingly refers to as a car," he said without greeting. "What the devil are you doing here, Sister Joan?"

"I've a perfect right to be here. I do teach here, you know? Anyway I thought it possible there might be something in one of the children's desks that might help—"

"We already looked," he said.

"When?"

"When Sister—the little nun who looks like a rabbit was deputizing for you."

"Sister David and she's very efficient. She's also a Latin scholar."

"Thanks for the reference." He let amusement creep into his smile. "Seriously, did you fancy that we wouldn't look here?"

"I didn't think—and Sister David never mentioned it."

"Does Sister David have to report to you?" he enquired.

"No, of course not." She frowned, thinking that Mother Dorothy might have mentioned the fact that the desks had already been searched, or had she thought that Sister Joan might find something the police had overlooked? More probably she had decided to let her come here in the hope that it might assuage her restlessness.

"We found nothing you wouldn't find in any school," he told her. "I take it that you haven't either?"

"Not a thing," she admitted.

"You've been making notes." He stooped to the wastepaper basket and smoothed out the paper.

"Amateur stuff," she said uncomfortably.

"But quite acute. Have the kids been unnaturally good?"

"Like angels. Very unnatural."

"Any ideas why?"

"Nothing to speak of."

She hadn't the right to point him in any particular direction.

"What's this about 'evil'?"

"Old Hagar up at the camp and Timothy's father both commented, independently, that they were conscious of the presence of evil. I suppose you don't believe in that?"

"You can't be a policeman and not believe in the reality of evil," he answered sombrely. "Man is a sick animal, Sister Joan. Make no mistake about that."

"And can also rise near to the angels," she said.

"You're an idealist, Sister." He smiled at her in a companionable fashion. "Also it may not be such a good idea for you or any of the community to go wandering alone in lonely places. I'm only assuming the two deaths are connected but the *modus operandi* was different in each case. So why not drive back to the convent and do—whatever nuns do all day?"

"I have some visits to make first. Sergeant, have you seen Padraic Lee?"

"Not this morning. Why?"

"He is very probably waiting for you down at the station then. His little girl found a heavy candlestick this morning, flung on the edge of the camp. She assumed it was scrap metal and took it to the wagon."

"He brought it to the station?" he asked sharply.

"He didn't know that anything had happened to Sister Margaret. Tabitha—his daughter is busily cleaning the candlestick up."

"Damn and blast!" he exploded.

"Detective Sergeant Mill!"

"Sorry, Sister Joan, but it's enough to make a saint swear. I'd better get down there at once. How did you happen to know?"

"Mr. Lee was driving past and saw the convent car."

"Get your visiting done," he said curtly, "and then get back to the convent."

" 'Get thee to a nunnery?' " she queried with a flash of mischief.

"That's the burden of it, Sister. Thanks for the information."

He went out, and she sat for a moment listening to the car drive away. He had taken her paper with him. She wondered if her own list of queries had stirred anything in his mind, or did he see her as a meddling amateur?

There had been another question she hadn't written down. The oddly sinister little rhyme that Samantha had produced for the homework task lingered like a bad taste.

They say daffodils are trumpets.
I say daffodils are strumpets,
And lads are bad and girls black pearls
And little roses full of worms.

In the deserted classroom the words had a chilling ring. She shivered slightly and hurried to lock up and get into the car.

Driving up to the greenway she thrust down the doubts that were crowding into her head. Ought she to have mentioned the rhyme to Detective Sergeant Mill? Did she have the right to direct his thoughts towards people who might be completely innocent? Children often went through a morbid phase when they were nearing puberty.

She parked below the crest in a dip of the land that effectively concealed the car from any casual glance. On Saturdays people often went out shopping or into town. She would have her words ready should it prove otherwise with the Olives.

"I'm very sorry to trouble you but I suppose you have heard of the very tragic event early this morning at the convent. I was wondering if you would care to give something towards a wreath for Sister Margaret?''

In daylight the big house lost its sinister aspect and became a large, bleak stone building that needed repointing and painting. She walked up to the front door and pulled the bell rope vigorously, hearing the echoing jangle within the house. Nobody came to open the door; no head poked out of a window. She rang the bell again with the same result and then walked slowly round to the back.

Here was a yard with a wash house and line. There was a washing-machine in the wash house, its gleaming white incongruous against the dirty whitewashed walls.

The back door was locked. Sister Joan scowled at it. When one contemplated action it was frustrating to be defeated by an inanimate object.

"The coal chute?'' She asked herself the question aloud as she looked around. There was no coal shute but there was another door, its surface pitted with woodworm, its padlock not completely secured.

If I hadn't entered the religious life I'd have made a splendid burglar, she decided, wrenching the padlock open and pulling at the door.

Steep steps led into blackness and the air was musty. The opening of the door admitted sufficient light to reveal another door at the bottom. She went down cautiously, glad that the grey habit of her Order reached only to the ankles and didn't trail on the ground. The door at the bottom of the stairs creaked when she turned the knob and pushed it ajar.

This was the cellar which was unsafe according to what the Olives had said. She hoped the day's adventure wouldn't end with herself buried under a pile of rubble.

So far, and making allowances for her limited vision in the deep gloom, everything seemed solid enough.

There was nothing there but a small, bare, very grubby cellar, with a further flight of stairs leading up to the ground floor. She mounted the stairs and opened the door, finding herself in the corridor that led past the main staircase into the front hall.

This was the door from which the new au pair, Jan Heinz, had emerged on the evening she and Sister Margaret had come visiting. She went to the foot of the stairs, looking up, listening to her own heartbeats in the silence of the house.

Then she was climbing the stairs, uncomfortably aware that the fact nothing in the rule specifically forbade the Daughters of Compassion to break into empty houses, was no excuse at all. Only her motive mitigated her fault.

There were numerous bedrooms, most of them unfurnished. The one she immediately identified as Samantha's had had some trouble taken over it. Fresh pink and white paper covered the walls and there were pink curtains at the windows. The furniture was white.

A pretty room for a cherished only child. With a feeling of shame at her own prying she opened the wardrobe door. Clothes hung on padded hangers, drawers at the side held neat piles of underwear. A long bookcase contained the familiar children's classics.

I am behaving abominably, she thought. Nothing justifies this prying.

At the back of the wardrobe behind a row of shoes was a neat weekend case. Lifting it out she clicked up the latch and stared, with a feeling less of surprise than of inevitability at the candles and the bunch of browned and limp daffodils, and the two plastic bottles of water.

Samantha had stolen these items from the church? Why?

What possible value could these things have? They were consecrated by virtue of the blessing conferred on everything in the chapel, but the child could have asked for them openly if she'd wanted them. Sister Joan reached in and picked up a prayer card, decorated with a sentimental Madonna and Child. The sentence on the back was in Samantha's round hand.

Please, dear God, protect my chastity. Amen.

A child of eleven praying that her chastity be protected? Why? The things taken from the chapel suddenly acquired a new and poignant significance. They were protective devices, shields against fear.

The sound of a car in the drive below brought her to her feet. The Olives were back. She dropped the prayer card back, closed the suitcase and thrust it behind the shoes, sped along the corridor and down the stairs, whisking through the cellar door just as a key grated in the lock of the front door. Muffled voices sounded and footsteps.

The gloom of the cellar was intense after the daylight of the upper storey. She forced herself to go slowly down the stairs, one hand out to trail along the wall. She was at the bottom when the wall yielded to her palm, moving inwards as if it were a living creature.

A door, her commonsense told her. She groped automatically for a light switch and jumped with relief as light flooded the chamber in which she stood. This part of the cellars had been whitewashed and the floor covered with rush matting. Shelves on the wall held video tapes and albums, and suitcases were piled against the wall opposite.

A storeroom? She took out one of the albums and skirted the protruding edge of a suitcase.

Photographs were neatly arranged in plastic covers within the album. Her eyes were riveted to the page at which she had opened it. A feeling of sick horror flooded her being as the subject matter penetrated her reluctant understanding. She had heard of pornography, but had never, even before entering the religious life, seen anything that could be construed as more than mildly erotic. These carefully posed photographs were so sick that her mind rebelled against the knowledge that human beings had posed for and taken them.

Her hands felt dirty. She dropped the album and stumbled into the outer cellar, wanting only to get out into the fresh air and sunlight. The yard was deserted. She went through a side gate, stood retching for a moment, and then set off at a swerving run across the greenway to where she had left the car.

TWELVE

✠ ✠ ✠

The police station had its usual air of understated bustle. Sister Joan, hurrying in, was greeted by the same desk sergeant she had seen before.

"Good afternoon, Sister. No more bad news, I hope? You've had your fair share of it up at the convent, I'd say."

"Is Detective Sergeant Mill here?" she asked.

"What can I do for you, Sister?" He put his head in at the door.

"May I speak to you for a few moments?" she asked tensely.

"Be my guest." He held open the door politely.

This wasn't the office where she'd had her fingerprints taken but a smaller room with filing cabinets stacked against one wall and a desk on which a photograph of two small boys held pride of place.

"Your sons?" She took the chair he indicated.

"Brian and Kevin. My name's Alan."

"Detective Sergeant Mill," she said, not availing herself of the implied invitation, "you must go at once to the Olives' house and search it. The two of them—Clive and

Julia Olive, are earning their living from child pornography. That's against the law.''

"I know that, Sister." He had seated himself opposite her. "How do you come to know about this? Did the Olives confide in you or show you their collection or something?''

"Not exactly." She flushed slightly. "I drove over to the Olives but they were out, so I—I went in. Into the house.''

"The door was open and you waited for them in the sitting-room?''

"I got in," she said with dignity, "through the cellar.''

"You broke in.''

"I broke nothing," she said austerely. "There was a padlock on the cellar door that hadn't been properly fastened. I went in that way.''

"To—investigate?'' He lifted an eyebrow.

"I thought it was an opportunity," she defended herself. "I only went into Samantha's room. There was a suitcase at the back of her wardrobe with candles, dead flowers and two plastic bottles of water—I'd guess holy water—in it. And a prayer card asking God to protect her chastity.''

"The items pinched from your chapel.''

"Not the prayer card. She must have bought that somewhere. Anyway I heard the family returning so I nipped down into the cellar again and came out that way. The cellar's been sectioned off. There are shelves full of video tapes and albums of the most sickening photographs you could imagine. Quite clearly he isn't writing a book at all. He and his wife are in the pornography trade.''

"You brought samples with you?''

"Sam—? Well, no, I didn't." Her flush deepened. "I was so shocked that I just—I think I dropped the album and came away as quickly as I could. I'd left the car some distance from the house so I drove straight here.''

"Leaving the evidence behind?''

"You can go and search the house now that I've told you. You can get a search warrant, acting on information received.''

"Sister Joan, it is now mid afternoon on Saturday,'' he said, heavily patient. "The local magistrates won't be around until Monday and the Chief Constable through whom I must request a search warrant will need more cause than the unsupported word of someone who hasn't any evidence and made her discovery when she was in the course of committing a felony herself.''

"That's the silliest thing I ever heard,'' she said.

"Nevertheless it's the way things work. You'd be the first one to scream about violation of human rights if we could obtain search warrants at a moment's notice and barge in anywhere.''

"I really did see what I told you.''

"I don't doubt it, Sister—is that your real name—Joan? Or did they give you a new one?''

"I was baptised Joan. What are you going to do about the Olives?''

"I'll go and see the Chief Constable and see if I can talk him round. It might help if you could explain why you drove over to the Olives in particular. Why not the Holts or the Penglows?''

"It was the poem.''

"What poem?'' he demanded.

"Samantha Olive handed it in as part of her homework. The children had to write about their favourite flowers. Samantha wrote—*They say daffodils are trumpets, I say daffodils are strumpets, and lads are bad and girls black pearls, and little roses full of worms.*''

"Not exactly a nursery rhyme," he said dryly. "Did she compose it herself?"

"She says that she did. She is very bright for her age. I didn't question her about it too closely. Perhaps I should have done."

"You think she's been exposed to this pornographic racket?"

"I think she's aware of it. I think that's why she stole the things from the chapel—to protect herself. Am I going to be charged with—a felony?"

"I will endeavour," he said wryly, "to keep your name out of it. However it will be Monday before any warrant'll be forthcoming. In the meantime I'd be grateful if you'd keep your recent exploits under your veil. No sense in alerting anybody."

"There is general confession today," she said doubt-fully. "I reckon that I can postpone saying anything."

"I'd be grateful. I'd also be grateful if you'd stay in the convent for a few days and stop dashing off on impulse."

"Did you get the candlestick?"

"That wretched child—Tabitha? had washed and pol-ished it," he said. "However there's no doubt in my mind that it was used to hit Sister Margaret. Whoever did it swung it by the base. The shape corresponds with the wound. There wouldn't have been much bleeding."

A cold shiver rippled through her at the picture his words conjured up. Sister Margaret, halfway through the door into the visitors' parlour, the assailant turning and striking. Had that been her last conscious thought? The person she had admitted turning to reveal the face of a devil?

"She'll be released to you this evening," he said more gently, watching her face.

"Yes. Thank you, Sergeant Mill."

At the door she stopped suddenly, her expression changing as she exclaimed, "I wonder what happened to it!"

"To what?" He had moved to open the door.

"The candle in the candlestick. There are always candles in the candlesticks. They are lit during evening prayers and then snuffed out—that's Sister David's task. Your men didn't find it in the chapel?"

He shook his head.

"Was there anything special about it?"

"It was thinner and taller than the candles we light before the Lady Altar. It was exactly like the other candle. They were both well burned down. Usually they are replaced on Saturday after prayers ready for Sunday."

"The killer probably took the candle away with him."

"As a souvenir?" she asked bitterly. "How could anyone have hurt someone like Sister Margaret? She was a good woman—a truly good woman."

"The angle of the wound shows it was inflicted from above and in front. Sister Margaret was five feet four inches, so he has to be taller than that. Thank you for the information you gave me, Sister. I can trust you not to go breaking in anywhere else, I hope?"

"I promise you," she said, and went out. She had not promised not to visit anywhere else. Getting into the car she drove away in the direction of the camp.

The visit of the police had left its mark. The usual bustle was missing with women huddled in small knots about the steps of their wagons and the men watching her as she alighted from the car. Tabitha with Edith tagging behind her emerged from the Lee wagon, and came trotting over.

"Good morning, Sister Joan. Have you come to see Dad? He had to go and get some medicine for Mum. She's feeling poorly."

"I'm very sorry to hear it," Sister Joan said.

"Oh, she never feels very good when she's been on the bottle," Tabitha informed her cheerfully. "They're going to let Petroc's daddy out of clink—"

"Gaol, dear."

"Yes, the gaol," Tabitha said, unabashed. "That policeman came and took away the silver candlestick I found. I don't like him."

"He's just doing his job."

"I polished it ever so nice." The small face was wistful. "I'd have got good marks for that. Maybe I'd have won the prize. Like Petroc did, only he got dead."

"What prize?" Sister Joan spoke sharply, too sharply. The child wriggled and shuffled her feet.

"Samantha's mum and dad give prizes to the best children," Edith piped up. "It's a secret. If we tell anyone something awful will happen, so we have to be good all the time."

"Who told you that?" She tried to sound no more than casually interested.

"It's a secret," Tabitha said, giving her sister a dig in the ribs. "We mustn't tell."

"Surely you can tell me?"

"If we tell we might end up dead," Tabitha said.

"Petroc ended up dead," Edith said thoughtfully. "I don't think he told. We thought he'd won the prize because he's been very, very good."

"What is the prize?" Sister Joan asked. The palms of her hands were wet.

"We get to drink real champagne," Tabitha said, lowering her voice, "and we get our photos took."

"Have you already—?" Her heart felt ready to burst.

"Petroc won the prize first," Edith said. "He was go-ing to tell us all about it, but he never came back."

"He went to Heaven," Tabitha announced.

"Yes. Yes, he did," Sister Joan said, and hugged the little girl almost fiercely.

Study hour had already begun. She rose, wondering if she ought to warn the children to stay close to the wagon, but Conrad came past with a bucket of water, calling as he came, " 'Afternoon, Sister Joan. Now you two stay where I can keep an eye on you until your dad gets back."

She drove back to the convent with speculations buzz-ing in her brain.

"You were a long time, Sister." The prioress had emerged from the kitchen as she went in the back way.

"I'm sorry, Mother Dorothy, but there was quite a lot to do. Shall I tell you about—?"

"Not just now, Sister." The voice was firm. "You had better hurry to your studies. I am expecting some inter-esting conclusions from you on the subject of the four branches of the rule."

"Yes, Mother Dorothy. Mother Dorothy—?"

"What is it, Sister?"

"I believe that it's time to inform the detective sergeant about Kiki Svenson. It may help him obtain a search war-rant. To the Olives' house."

"I will telephone immediately. Your studies, Sister."

Poverty, chastity, obedience, compassion. She went slowly to her cell, the words revolving in her mind. For a religious chastity included celibacy, but chastity itself was not always celibate just as celibacy was not always sterile. It was the damming up and diverting of the sexual instinct in order to bear spiritual fruit. Chastity was innocence and not ignorance; it was powerful and not weakly. And of all the rule it was the branch most vulnerable to temptation when one was young and spirited.

The bell for Benediction sounded before she had composed her ideas into the outline of an essay. Going downstairs, filing into the chapel, she felt the shock of loss as she saw the open coffin before the altar. The wound on Sister Margaret's temple was hidden by her coif and there was a faint dreaming look upon her face.

"Sisters." Mother Dorothy was on her feet. "As you can see our beloved Sister Margaret has been brought home to lie among us until her burial on Monday. I say she is here but of course she is even now giving an account of herself before the Divine Throne—"

No, she is not! Sister Joan thought on a surge of rebellion. She is probably having a little chat with her Dear Lord, face to face, making Him laugh with her anecdotes about cooking and getting fish from Padraic Lee. She bowed her head and began to intone the prayers for the dead with her sisters.

"There will be no recreation tonight," Mother Dorothy was saying. "We shall eat our supper which the postulants have kindly prepared under the supervision of Sister Teresa. Then we will have Benediction and then take our turns at watching with Sister Margaret. Sister Katherine and Sister David from eight to ten, Sister Martha and myself from ten to midnight, Sister Perpetua and Sister Teresa from midnight until two,—what is it, Sister Gabrielle?"

"I wonder if Sister Mary Concepta and I could take the earlier vigil, Reverend Mother."

"I had not expected—" Mother Dorothy began, then nodded. "Of course you too will wish to keep vigil. Very well. You and Sister Mary Concepta immediately after Benediction from eight to ten, Sisters Katherine and David from ten to midnight, Sister Martha and myself from midnight until two, Sister Perpetua and Sister Teresa from two until four, and Sister Hilaria and Sister Joan from four until six. After that our two postulants will watch until Father Malone comes to offer mass. Sister Marie and Sister Elizabeth, I think it would be wiser if you and Sister Hilaria were to sleep in the main house tonight. Sister Katherine will put blankets on the beds in the two empty cells and Sister Hilaria may occupy my cell since I will not be sleeping at all. Thank you, Sisters.''

They filed out and up into the refectory. This had once been a drawing-room in the days when the Tarquin family had owned the estate and it retained its noble proportions, its gilded cornices and picture rail. Double doors that could be fastened back to make a huge ballroom separated it from the recreation room. The arrangements of flowers, the gilt-edged mirrors and spindly-legged chairs that must once have graced it were replaced by two long tables and benches with a chair for the prioress. When she had first joined the community the novices had eaten with the professed sisters. Under Mother Dorothy's more stringent interpretation of the rules the novices now took their meals in their own quarters, but this evening they sat at the side table, blue-bonneted heads bowed.

The prioress stepped to the lectern and began to read a synopsis of the lives of various saints named Margaret—a happy touch, Sister Joan thought, and one that Sister Margaret would have approved. She ate the dish of lentils that the postulants had cooked and listened to the legend of Margaret of Cortona who had been swallowed and vomited up by a dragon, St. Margaret of Hungary whose apron had been filled with roses and St. Margaret of Scotland who had been a faithful wife and mother as well as a saint.

Sister Margaret would have enjoyed tonight's reading.

Supper ended. The grace was intoned and the last glass of water drained.

"Sister Joan." Mother Dorothy beckoned her. "I telephoned Detective Sergeant Mill and was fortunate enough to get straight through to him just before Sister Margaret was brought home. He thanked me for the information about Kiki Svenson and said he would follow it up."

"Thank you, Reverend Mother."

"He also informed me that the weapon used was indeed the missing candlestick from the altar. Apparently it has yielded no clues. I will ask Father Malone to cleanse and bless it when it has been returned to us. That is all, Sister."

"No general confession," Sister Gabrielle whispered as they went out. "Well, there'll be a double ration to remember next week."

Sister Joan nodded, her heart sinking. General confession, she thought wryly, was becoming more and more of an ordeal.

Going down again into the chapel for Benediction she found the questions revolving in her mind again. Had Petroc's death been an accident? If so then why bring him to the chapel? Why—?

The telephone rang in the prioress's parlour, shrilling through the corridor.

"Sister Joan, be so good as to answer the telephone," Mother Dorothy turned to say.

"Yes, Reverend Mother." For an instant she had almost expected Sister Margaret to bustle across the hall.

The voice at the other end said tentatively, "Is the convent, ya?"

"Kiki Svenson? Yes, yes, this is the convent. Sister Joan speaking." The relief was so immense that her legs felt weak. "You got my message?"

"From the lady, ya. I cannot return. I ring to tell you that. I ran away from that bad house and hide myself in the home of a friend for some time, in case they find me."

"Miss Svenson, can you telephone the police? Ask for a Detective Sergeant Mill. I can give you the number—"

"No police. My family will be—in scandal if they know where I work—"

"Miss Svenson, a child has been killed. Please telephone the Bodmin police. It really is—"

There was a sharp click on the other end as Kiki Svenson hung up. Sister Joan stared at the instrument in impotent fury for a moment, then whirled round and went in as near a run as made no difference into the chapel.

"O salutaris hostia." The sweet, sexless voices of the community rose in unison. After Benediction came the grand silence, the vigil in the chapel—no time to say anything. The rule was heavy on her heart as she knelt and joined in the chant.

At the blessing she tried to signal with her eyes to the prioress that she needed permission to speak, but Mother Dorothy sprinkled her with the cold drops of water without looking at her. The prioress looked tired and worn, her shoulders more hunched than usual. From now on she would cling desperately to the routine of convent life, would regard the two deaths as an intrusion into the calm of the enclosure.

In her cell she took off her coif and veil and covered her shorn dark head with her white nightcap, and lay down on her bed in the attitude recommended for sleeping—flat on her back with clasped hands.

"If you should die during your sleep you will leave your body in the appropriate position for burial," her first novice mistress had instructed her.

Lying thus made her feel too much like Sister Margaret

and Petroc, stretched before the altar. She twisted on to her side, her fingers automatically clasping her rosary as she began to tell her beads, the silent words dropping like the cool water of the blessing into the darkness. Her last thought as she drifted into an exhausted sleep was the guilty conviction that for praying one ought to make the effort to get down on one's knees—on one's knees—on one's—

A hand shook her awake: Sister Perpetua's large, capable hand. She nodded and sat up, rubbing her eyelids which felt gritty for lack of proper slumber. Dawn filtered through the blind at the window.

Replacing coif and veil, kneeling briefly to give silent thanks for the gift of another day, thrusting aside the sudden irritable notion that not every day was a gift to be accepted with gratitude, she rose finally and went into the corridor and down to the chapel.

Sister Hilaria was already on her knees by the coffin, her eyes dreaming into her private celestial worlds. Death held no terrors for people like Sister Hilaria, Sister Joan thought, dropping to her knees beside her, letting the solemn quiet wash over her.

The loud ringing of the rising bell made her jump violently. For one disorientated moment she looked at Sister Margaret and wondered how on earth she could manage to be in two places at once. Then her common sense reasserted itself. Obviously Mother Dorothy had instructed one of the others, probably Sister Teresa, to ring it.

"Christ is risen," Sister Hilaria said.

"Thanks be to God." Sister Joan made the customary rejoinder that marked the end of the grand silence.

"How strange it seems," Sister Hilaria murmured, "not to hear Sister Margaret saying those words. Always so cheerful. Striding across to the postulants' quarters as if the world had been new created. Such a pretty singing voice.''

''I didn't know that Sister Margaret could sing.''

''Who? Oh, no, Sister, I meant my postulant, Sister Marie. She has a very pretty voice and sings out her responses like a little bird. Not that she makes a very good cook. I was teasing her a little about not even being able to read a recipe—though the lentils were very tasty. But Sister Margaret seemed quite struck by my remark.''

Sister Joan opened her mouth but never found out what she had intended to say. Sister Hilaria was lost in her devotions again, lost in the only world where she felt at ease, the only world where her mind didn't wander vaguely from subject to subject but could centre itself firmly on the source.

Rising, she went swiftly to the side door, passed through to the outer door, unlocked it and went out into the morning. The feeling that something was rising to a climax was very strong in her. Every instinct told her against all reason to hurry.

There was no time to ask permission to use the car. On the other hand she could ride Lilith at any time. Neither would she be breaking her promise to Detective Sergeant Mill by breaking into anywhere new. She had already broken into the Olive residence.

Lilith whickered a welcome as she hurried into the stable. The old horse had missed her customary exercise. It was a pity, she thought, that she hadn't had time to slip on her new jeans, but if she had gone upstairs she would have been caught up in the normal Sunday morning routine.

Mounting, she tapped Lilith smartly across her broad back and set off at a gallop down the drive. Since she had been foolish enough to leave the evidence behind then she had a clear duty to go and collect it again before the Olives took fright and disposed of it, and she wanted to think as she rode, of Sister Hilaria's vague, disconnected thought patterns. She wanted very badly to think about that.

THIRTEEN

✠ ✠ ✠

Lilith submitted placidly to being tethered to a tree in the hollow below the greenway. As she made her way up the slopes towards the house Sister Joan felt the beauty of the early morning unfold about her. Long streaks of fine white mist wreathed about the bushes and were glinted with silver by the first light. To think of child murder, child pornography on such a morning seemed like a small blasphemy. Both smeared dirt over the chastity of a new spring day.

The house was silent, curtains drawn. Going round to the back yard she felt a definite relief that the Olives didn't keep a dog.

The door that led down into the cellar was still not properly bolted. Presumably in such an isolated spot they had no fear of intruders. She recalled the way in which she had been neatly deflected from being shown over the house with the bland statement that the cellars were unsafe. No, the Olives felt quite secure in leaving their obscene collection down below.

The faint light that filtered down the steps into the cellar had about it a greenish, sickly quality as if something down there altered its essence. She took a deep breath, telling herself not to be an imaginative idiot and went down, trusting that her guardian angel hadn't slept in late.

The inner door at the foot of the stairs leading up to the main part of the house was locked. She stared at its smooth varnished surface with dismay. Well, locks meant keys. Keys were generally kept—where? Perhaps on a key ring in the kitchen or in the study—if there was a study. She hoped that nobody in the Olive household got up early on a Sunday morning.

The ground floor passage was dim and chilly. Standing in the angle between staircase and wall she strained her ears for some sound but there was nothing. At least the place seemed to have fitted carpets everywhere which muffled her light step. It would also have muffled the sound of Sister Margaret's rosary as it broke from its mooring at her belt and slid down to the carpet. She was certain that this was where Sister Margaret had lost her rosary, had been subconsciously aware of its slipping down to the floor. In the kitchen with Sister Hilaria and the two postulants, teasing them about their inability to follow a recipe, her mind must surely have jumped to the one house they had visited that evening where no food had been consumed, no recipes talked about or given. At least her enforced silence because prayers were about to begin hadn't cost her her life. She had been killed for some other reason.

She went into the big drawing-room and looked round without much hope. It was very unlikely that any keys were kept here. The room behind was smaller, lined with shelves on which gaudily covered paperbacks resided. There was a flat-topped desk near the door. She risked switching on the table lamp on the desk and cautiously tried the first drawer. It was unlocked, almost filled with neat bundles of cheque stubs. There was no sign, she thought cynically, of anyone engaged in the writing of a book. Neither were there any keys.

She turned off the light and went out into the hall again. Around the edges of the curtains the light was strengthening. There was need for haste. A dining-room and the cavernous, green painted kitchen yielded nothing to the casual gaze. Everything was faintly shabby and dusty, though certainly not as grime encrusted as Sister Margaret had mentioned. But then Sister Margaret had been picking up the spiritual dirt that corrupted the place, she reflected. Sister Margaret, with her bustling common sense, her cheerful humility had travelled far along the road to spiritual sensitivity.

The prospect of mounting the stairs, of going into bedrooms where people might well be stirring in preparation for a full awakening to the day, was beyond her courage. She went back into the drawing-room and stood uncertainly, under the gaze of Samantha's enlarged photograph over the mantelshelf, trying to think what to do next. The Olives weren't stupid people. The death of Sister Margaret following so closely on the death of the child must alert them to the possibility of a house to house search. By the time Detective Sergeant Mill got his warrant every video and photo album would be gone from the cellar. Probably burnt piece by piece in the furnace that serviced the huge radiators that kept the house so warm. The house was cool now, more bearable. People who lived abroad generally felt the cold when they returned to England. That might be a possibility to mention to the sergeant when she saw him next.

"Sister Joan, oh, how lovely to see you!"

She swung round, her heart jumping into her mouth and met Samantha's uplifted gaze. The child had on shortie pyjamas patterned with rosebuds and her feet were bare.

"Good morning, Samantha." What a blessing the automatic courtesies were! "I came to see your parents."

And please God, don't let the child think to enquire how I got in.

"They're asleep," Samantha said. "I've been lying awake, thinking. How old do you have to be before you can become a nun?"

"At least eighteen, dear. Until then people often aren't sure what they want to do with their lives."

"The Little Flower did."

"St. Therese of Lisieux was a saint," Sister Joan said, wondering how many naive young girls fancied they could emulate a saint whose sentimental prettiness concealed an indomitable will.

"Maybe I could get to be a saint," Samantha said wistfully. "It must be very safe in a convent."

"Yes, well—" Sister Joan hesitated, then plunged. "You took the things from the convent chapel in order to protect yourself, didn't you?"

"I know that it was wrong." In the strengthening light the child's sallow little face had flushed a dull red. "I could have asked for them, but if I'd asked then my parents might have got to hear of it. They don't believe in God or things like that. I know that I should have asked, but you used to keep the convent chapel unlocked all night and I don't mind long walks. My mother and father—they don't pay much attention to me. They feed me and clothe me and buy me nice, expensive things, but they don't often sit down and talk to me. When we were in India they left me with an ayah all the time and she was so stupid you wouldn't believe. And then we came back to London and they started—well, their business and then they moved here. Daddy said that it would be—more prudent, to lie low for a bit until he could arrange the sale of—but I'm not supposed to talk about that. I'm not supposed even to know about that, but I do know and I get scared, Sister Joan. I get so scared.''

"Everybody gets scared sometimes.'' Sister Joan moved to the window and drew back the curtain. "Is that why you killed Sister Margaret, Samantha?''

"What?'' The child stared at her. "How could I—? Sister, that's a terrible thing to say.''

"It was a terrible thing to do,'' Sister Joan said. "You were afraid that she might remember where she dropped the rosary, weren't you? So you went back to the chapel very early in the morning. It was locked. You said just now that we 'used to leave the door open.' Used to, Samantha. How did you know we'd started locking it? Nobody has ever made any announcement about it.''

"I guess that someone must have told me,'' Samantha said.

"I don't think so.'' Sister Joan kept her eyes steadily on the plain little face. "But it will be easy enough to check. We can go up to your room right now and take a look in the suitcase at the back of your wardrobe. I reckon we'll find the candle there. The one that fell out of the candlestick when you were trying to get away from Sister Margaret.''

"Well, you're wrong, Sister. You're just wrong! That candle was nearly burnt down and it didn't match any of the others,'' Samantha said triumphantly. "So I threw it away. I just tossed it into the furnace here. I'd like to toss everything into the furnace—all the rotten pictures and the videos and the—dirty, fucking—oh, I beg your pardon, Sister. That was a very bad word to use.''

"Was it because of all that that you killed Petroc?'' She

marvelled inwardly at the calmly conversational tone of her voice.

"Petroc was a beautiful boy," Samantha said, licking her lips with her pointed little tongue. "I knew that sooner or later my parents would see him and invite him to the house and give him the sugared wine with the stuff in it, and then take photographs. In India they used to pick up street children you know. They gave them sweets afterwards and let them go, but people started asking questions. Damned rumour-mongers, Daddy said. So we came back to England but the children were all spoilt anyway. I didn't want the ones at the school to be spoilt. Not any of them."

"You saw Petroc swimming with Hagar."

"They looked so—clean," Samantha said sadly. "I didn't want them to be spoilt. So I told Petroc that he'd won the prize and he came to the house and I gave him the sugared wine. It wasn't to kill him. I never wanted to kill anybody. Honestly, Sister. But he liked the taste and he went on drinking it and then he went all limp and cold and water ran out of him and I didn't know what to do."

"Who took him to the chapel?" Sister Joan asked.

"Daddy came down into the cellar," Samantha told her. "He said not to worry, that he'd see to everything. And he took him to the chapel. It was the best place for him. He hadn't been spoilt, you see."

"That was where you wanted your daddy to take him, was it?"

"Oh, Daddy usually does what I want," Samantha said. "He knows that I'd tell on him if he didn't. About the photographs, I mean."

"And you put the rosary in his pocket."

"It slipped down on to the hall carpet from her belt when you came over that night. Jan picked it up and I took it. I thought it might come in useful. Jan is very stupid, you know. He doesn't speak any English and he will drive me just anywhere I want to go. I guess it's because he sleeps in the same bed as Mummy and he wants to keep me sweet.''

''Kiki?'' Sister Joan said in a whisper.

''Oh, she was more stupid,'' Samantha said contemptuously. ''She saw the photographs and she got scared and ran off in the middle of the night. She walked off. I daresay she got a lift or something on the main road.''

''You took the crucifix out of the chapel,'' Sister Joan said.

''I got Jan to drive me over,'' Samantha told her. ''He's so stupid; you just point him in the right direction and tell him what place to stop in. I thought it would be very big protection to have the crucifix but it was terribly heavy and so I went and sat in that box—''

''The confessional.''

''When I heard someone coming. When you went out again I put it back and went back to the car. It was parked right by the wall but you never noticed it.''

''And then you came back—''

''I never came to hurt any of the sisters,'' Samantha broke in. ''I thought it would be nice to have something really powerful from the chapel and the crucifix was too heavy. I got up terribly early and walked all the way there, but the door was locked. That's a bad thing to do, to lock people out of a chapel. I started rattling at the door and suddenly Sister Margaret opened it. She started to ask me what I wanted but I ran past her and grabbed the candlestick. That was heavy too but not as heavy as the crucifix. I had to yank at her veil to get past her again, but she wouldn't let me go. She grabbed at me and fell on her knees and that made me bigger than her so I turned round and hit her. I wanted her to let go, silly cow—oh, pardon me, Sister. That isn't a very respectful way to talk about a nun.''

''You picked up the candle,'' Sister Joan said carefully.

''And then I ran,'' Samantha said simply. ''I went by way of the camp and threw the candlestick there. I had my gloves on. You have to wear gloves when you're taking things, you know. That's very important, I kept the candle but it didn't match the others so I put it in the furnace.''

''You're very bright for your age.'' She kept her voice level, mildly interested.

''Yes, I have a very high IQ and I think that's nice. It would make me very useful in a convent.''

''So bright that I can't understand why you didn't ask someone for help if you were frightened about what was going on. People listen to children these days. There is a Help Line you can ring.''

''But if I'd done that,'' Samantha said, ''the welfare people would have taken me away. I like having pretty things and my own room and being able to wander about without people going on at me about where I get to and what I do. And it would be very wrong to tell on your parents. Only, sometimes—'' Her brow creased and she hugged herself as if an icy wind had ruffled the borders of her rose-patterned pyjamas. ''Sometimes it's like there's another Samantha inside me that gets so frightened and wants to be safe. Isn't it funny, Sister?''

''No,'' said Sister Joan. ''No—it isn't very funny.''

''The point is,'' Samantha said, ''what are we going to do about it all. Was it you went into the cellar and dropped the photo album? I found it on the floor and I put it back. I didn't tell on you, Sister. And of course you can't tell on me.''

''What do you mean?''

"You're a nun and I just confessed to you. People can't tell what they hear in confession if they're nuns, can they? I heard that somewhere."

"Priests can't tell, Samantha. Priests are bound by the seal of the confessional. Confessions made to anyone else, even nuns, don't count. You're not a Catholic or you would understand that. I can tell. It's my duty to do so."

"But then I won't be able to go into a convent when I'm eighteen." Panic flashed into the small face. "I'll be safe in a convent and my chastity won't be spoilt. I can leave the other Samantha outside—"

"The other?"

"The one who goes out and picks the pretty children and invites them home for Daddy to play with while Mummy's in bed with someone or other. She likes pleasing her daddy because then he leaves her alone. Nobody really loves him, you see, because he's got a club foot just like the Devil. So the children have to be brought to him and then afterwards he and I watch the videos and sort through the photos, and then some of them get sold. But I didn't want it to be Petroc, Sister. He was a nice boy. Don't you think he was a nice boy? If he got dead then nobody could spoil him, could they?"

And Lucifer, thought Sister, wasn't a Dutch au pair but the child standing near to him when she and Sister Hilaria had stopped on their way to the dentist. The novice mistress had been referring in her usual, disconnected way to the child when she spoke of Lucifer. In the speech patterns of a woman whose mind was nearer heaven than earth had lain the answers to the questions.

"You are—a very sick little girl," she said slowly. "You have to understand that you are a very sick little girl, Samantha. You need—help. You need—"

In olden days they would have burned her at the stake,

recognizing evil in the flowerlike soul of a corrupted child. In these more enlightened times they called it sickness and treated it with medicine—or were these times more enlightened?

"I need to be protected," Samantha said. "I hoped you'd do it. That's why I wrote that little verse. I thought it might give you a clue, that it might help you to—stop me—stop the other Samantha, you see, and then I can go into the convent and be pure all my life. But you won't help me. You'll run off and tell on me, and then the welfare people will take me away. You're just a bitch, Sister Joan. A dried-up, frustrated old bitch—just like my daddy said. He laughs about you, Sister. You and that fat cow you brought with you to talk about stupid school projects. You're a—oh, excuse me. That really isn't very polite, is it?"

"Not in the least polite," said Detective Sergeant Mill as he pushed the door wider and entered the room.

Samantha had jerked around, staring at him. Then with a swift, convulsive movement, headed towards Sister Joan, burying her face in the grey skirt of the habit.

"Sergeant—" Sister Joan looked up into a face from which all disrespectful teasing had fled.

"You must detach yourself, Sister," he said.

"Yes. I know." She looked down with pity wrenching her heart and then spoke steadily. "Get up, Samantha. If you are going to enter the religious life you must learn to do as you're bidden by your superior in the religious life, you know."

A policewoman had come in. Somewhere in the house sounded a babble of voices, the thudding of feet.

Samantha lifted her head. Her cheeks were slightly flushed, her eyes shining.

"Yes, Sister," she said meekly, and rose, her smile widening as she glanced towards the detective. "They can't keep me for ever, can they, Sister? Not a child of eleven?''

"Take her down to the station," he said curtly to the policewoman. "Watch her. She's paranoid."

"Yes, Detective Sergeant. Come along, Samantha." The policewoman put out her hand.

"Don't touch me!" Samantha said sharply. "You look to me like the sort of woman who goes with men. Don't you touch me. I can walk all by myself."

Walking out, she looked back briefly as she reached the door and her face was filled with all the laughter of childhood.

"Your prioress was still up," he said to Sister Joan. "She saw you through the window, galloping off hell-for-leather across the moor and telephoned me. I'd just got back with the search warrant—"

"You got it then?"

"Kiki Svenson rang the station late last night with a garbled tale of having run off when she found out the sort of fun and games that's been going on here. I took a tip from you and came in via the cellar. I've got to get back to the station. There are charges to be made, arrangements—shall I run you back to the convent first?"

"I've tethered Lilith below the greenway. I need some fresh air."

"You look," he said as she rose shakily, "as if you need a stiff brandy."

"I think," she said, trying to smile, "that I've broken quite enough rules recently."

"I'll be along later today to fill in the pieces. Ride carefully, Sister Joan."

"Yes. Detective Sergeant."

She went past him into the hall. Police cars were driving away, two officers coming from the cellar with piles of videos and albums. A bewildered and beautiful Jan Heinz went past, protesting volubly in Dutch. Victim or willing accomplice? They were all, she thought, hurrying towards the gate victims of one kind or another.

FOURTEEN

✠ ✠ ✠

"It is rather difficult to know where to start, Sister Joan."
Mother Dorothy cupped her chin in her hand and frowned
at the younger woman.

"I have been greatly at fault, Reverend Mother," Sister
Joan said.

"You have certainly broken a great many rules—not
only the rule on which our Order is based but legal rules.
To enter a private house in such an unauthorized fashion
is really quite shocking. Think of the scandal if you had
been charged."

"Yes, Mother."

"If you had sought permission—but then you knew such
permission would not be given. So you went ahead and
followed your own instincts, forgetting that we lead a life
that is based not upon individual instinct but the moral
law. You did right to tell me in private. These matters are
not for general confession."

Sister Joan, on her knees, glanced up and caught a faint
quirk on her superior's grim mouth.

"The entire community would be scandalized," Mother
Dorothy was continuing. "I fear that your heart

frequently rules your head, Sister, and I also fear that you set up your own will too often against the will of the community. We can only be grateful that God turned your ill-considered actions to the solving of the crime.''

''Perhaps the end did justify the means?'' Sister Joan ventured.

''An excellent maxim for a Jesuit. You are not a Jesuit so spare me your clever comments.''

''Yes, Reverend Mother.''

''As to penance—your notion of rushing off to spend a period in retreat is simply a desire to escape. Who is going to run the school when you are gone? Sister David has quite sufficient to do already and I certainly cannot spare any of the others. What effect will it have upon your pupils with whom you had planned to do this project? They will already have lost two of their fellows and your sudden leaving will make them even more insecure.''

''I hadn't thought of that, Reverend Mother.''

''The trouble with you, Sister, is that you seldom do think. You rush into things. That is a sign of spiritual immaturity. This desire for retreat is an example of that. Selfish indulgence were you to undertake it at the present time. On the other hand you certainly need a period of self-examination. During the summer vacation might be arranged. At our retreat up in Scotland—for a period not exceeding one month.''

''Thank you, Reverend Mother.'' Sister Joan beamed at her.

''As for a more immediate penance—since a retreat cannot ever be considered such—you will not leave these premises save to go to the school until the end of the summer term. Is that absolutely clear? I put you on your honour.''

''Yes, Reverend Mother.''

"Then God bless you and give you more sense of what is fitting for a Daughter of our Order. Now go and let the detective sergeant in for he has just driven up beyond the window. Oh, and Sister—"

"Reverend Mother?"

"You are dealing with that particular temptation in a praiseworthy manner—so far. Remember that we do not lock ourselves away from human affection. We seek to transcend it. Show the detective sergeant in and then you may stay. Since you are involved you had better hear what he has to say."

"I hoped to get away sooner," he apologized as Sister Joan opened the door. "This has been a fair old day, Sister."

"Indeed it has, Sergeant. Please, come into the parlour. Reverend Mother is waiting."

He looked weary but satisfied.

"Detective Sergeant Mill, good afternoon." Mother Dorothy inclined her head slightly. "Sister Joan has told me part of what has happened. I find it unutterably shocking."

"Child abuse always is, Mother Dorothy," he said grimly.

"Was the child, Samantha—?" She paused, deep distaste on her face.

"Not physically. Thank you." He took the chair she indicated. "She was the bait as far as we have been able to ascertain. Julia Olive is singing like a canary—says her husband forced everything on her. She seems to have consoled herself with a string of young men and to have enjoyed the creature comforts his trade brought her while closing her eyes to what was going on. We're waiting for an interpreter so we can question the Heinz lad, but I'm personally convinced that he hadn't much to do with anything. He's far too recent on the scene and this appears to have been going on for years. They lived out in India after their marriage; then a couple of years back they moved to London where he built up a very lucrative little porno business until the Vice Squad starting nosing round and he came down here.''

''To taint the landscape,'' Mother Dorothy said.

''Well put, ma'am.'' He nodded approval. ''Now round here we have poaching, the odd break-in, senior school-kids getting hold of some grass—marijuana or sniffing glue, an occasional domestic killing—but on the whole we're a law-abiding community. I was transferred here nearly a year ago from Taunton and the situation's much the same there. Straight crime and not too much of that.''

''Have the Olives been charged?''

''With offences against the Public Decency Act. That'll hold them for the moment. We have to make enquiries in detail further afield before we can throw the book at them. Oh, I've entered in my report that we searched the house after 'information received.' That means that Sister Joan won't be required to give evidence. It'll be tacitly assumed that we got a tip off from the underworld.''

''Sister Joan would certainly not wish for any publicity,'' Mother Dorothy agreed. ''The child—?''

''Paranoid, though I've no doubt the psychiatrists will have some fancy new term for it.'' He grimaced briefly. ''She's chatting away about what she did to anyone who'll listen. Her parents let her wander about all over the place, no supervision. She insists that her father had nothing to do with Petroc Lee's death. She rigged it up, gave the boy the wine, sugared and doctored, and killed him by mistake. Clive Olive hasn't admitted any involvement as yet but it seems fairly clear that he found the body and drove

over to the convent with it. Left it in your lap, so to speak.
Macabre.''

''Very.'' She snapped off the word like a thread of cotton.

''She—Samantha Olive, I mean—had put the rosary she
found in the boy's pocket, but later on I think she started
to worry in case Sister Margaret remembered where she'd
dropped it. She came back to the chapel—she says to pray,
but the door was locked. She made a statement about
that.'' He reached into his pocket and took out a typed
paper. ''Here it is. We've only just got this since we had
to have a lawyer over before we could take it officially.
The lawyer advised her not to say anything, but nobody
could've stopped that little—lady from boasting of her exploits. Now, where is it?—yes, here we are—*I couldn't
get in and I started rattling the handle. Then Sister Margaret opened the door. She asked me what I wanted and I
said that I wanted to pray. Then she said, 'But you're the
Olive child, aren't you? Samantha? I would like a little
talk with you, dear.' I guessed she knew that I'd picked up
the rosary she lost so I ran past her and grabbed one of
the big candlesticks from the altar. She was by the door
still and she started towards me, but I tugged hard at her
veil and got past. She tried to grab me but she slipped and
fell on her knees. I hit her with the candlestick and she
just fell over. I picked up the candle and I ran. I thought
it was silly to keep the candlestick so I went home by way
of the Romany camp and threw it towards the scrapheap.
I put the candle in our furnace at home because it didn't
match the ones I already had. I like things to match nicely.
I think it's simply disgusting to be untidy.*''

''She will be committed to a mental home? Treated?''

''Certainly kept in protective custody—for other people's protection,'' he said wryly. ''I don't have much faith in these clever doctors, you know. Granted she had a rotten start with parents like those two but she's their flesh and blood, after all.''

"And evil is a reality that takes no account of chronological age." The prioress nodded gravely.

"I wondered—for my own satisfaction more than anything what alerted Sister Joan to the identity of the killer.''

"I really wasn't sure, Detective Sergeant Mill," she said. "All the little pieces were floating around and I couldn't fit them together. But then Sister Hilaria had made a comment when we were on our way to the dentist—we stopped off briefly at the gate of the old Druid place and Samantha came out with the Dutch boy. Sister Hilaria seemed to be looking at him and as we drove off she said she'd been thinking of Lucifer, so for a time I wondered if—but then I realized that Sister Hilaria speaks as her thoughts wander, without any apparently logical pattern. She could have been referring to Samantha.''

"Isn't Lucifer supposed to be male?" He cocked an impudent eyebrow.

"The angels are androgynous, Sergeant," she said primly.

"How dull for them. Also he was supposed to be beautiful—well, yes, that would fit. Samantha Olive is one of those children who may well grow up to be stunningly lovely. When she smiles—there's an other-worldly quality there.''

"Not," said the prioress, "a world with which I would care for any of my nuns to be intimately acquainted.''

"I reckon not. Well, ladies, that's about it. It'll be months before the case comes to court. Now I'd better be getting back. I've a report to write up.''

"We haven't offered you any tea or coffee," Mother Dorothy began.

"Nothing for me, thanks. We're awash with tea and coffee down at the station. You'll be at the boy's funeral tomorrow?"

"Sister Joan, Sister David and myself. In the afternoon Sister Margaret will be laid to rest in the convent enclosure. Her parents are staying in Bodmin—very nice people and naturally deeply upset."

"Well, I'm not a religious man," he said, "but I'd like to pay my respects in the chapel before I leave if that's all right with you."

"Sister Joan will escort you. Sister, relieve Sister Katherine for the next couple of hours."

"Sister Katherine?" He glanced questioningly at her as they left the parlour.

"She is our linen mistress," Sister Joan reminded him. "She does the most exquisite embroidery."

"You sounded envious."

"Only of her opportunities. I love embroidery myself but the rest of us are more useful doing plain sewing and knitting. Sometimes it is very good for our humility to hold our talents in abeyance for a time."

"If you ever say that again," he advised as they went into the chapel, "try to sound more convincing."

In the candlelit chapel Sister Katherine rose, gliding out with bowed head as Sister Joan made the gesture of dismissal.

"She looks very peaceful. The dead usually do," he said briefly.

"That's only her shell," Sister Joan said. "Sister Margaret is probably very busy at this moment elsewhere."

"I've enough problems in this world without worrying about the bare possibility there might be a next one. Too many responsibilities, too few pounds in my pay packet at the end of the month, a hefty mortgage, two boys to educate. I don't get on with my wife, Sister. Nothing tangible. Just mutual boredom and incompatibility.''

"I am very sorry, Detective Sergeant Mill. How good of you both to stay together, for the children.''

"We stay out of habit," he said briefly. "They're nice boys though. Mischievous.''

"Shall we say a prayer?'' she suggested.

"Say one for me, Sister. I was never very good at getting on my knees. She was a good woman was Sister Margaret—a good woman. And what about you now?''

"Me?'' She was startled into a question.

"I hope you didn't get into any trouble as a result of helping out. You're a very good woman yourself.''

"Oh, I'm not good at all,'' she assured him hastily. "Believe me, but I'm full of faults. I'll have to work pretty hard to eradicate them.''

"Here in the convent?''

"Wherever I am sent. In the summer I shall go into retreat in our Scottish house—I shall have a whole month completely alone to refresh my spirit.''

"On bread and water, I suppose? Medievalism.''

"Well, it won't be caviare,'' she said impishly. "But it will be a marvellous month. So peaceful and quiet with nothing to disturb the tranquillity.''

"I wouldn't care to make a bet on that, Sister.'' He sounded amused. "You and tranquillity don't mix very easily. Thank you for your help anyway. Say a prayer for me.''

Bending his head briefly in the direction of the altar he strode out into the world again.

Sister Joan heard the closing of the door but didn't turn her head. Her rosary in her fingers she had begun the gentle rhythm of her prayers.